# THE STORY OF ENID

## VOL. 2. OF THE CLANDESTINE EXPLOITS OF A WEREWOLF

BY

## EVELYN KLEBERT

**The Story of Enid**
Vol. 2. of The Clandestine Exploits of a Werewolf
By Evelyn Klebert

A Cornerstone Book
Published by Cornerstone Book Publishers

First Cornerstone Edition – 2025

Cornerstone Book Publishers
Hot Springs Village, AR
www.cornerstonepublishers.com

ISBN 978-1-61342-453-7

# Dedication

*For Michael,*
*The Reason I Write*
*Love Stories*

# Table of Contents

Ch. 1 Erin Holt ........................................................1

Ch. 2 Unexpected ...................................................12

Ch. 3 Darkness .......................................................18

Ch. 4 Before ...........................................................26

Ch. 5 Ethan ............................................................32

Ch. 6 Aftermath .....................................................38

Ch. 7 Enid ..............................................................43

Ch. 8 Forward ........................................................50

Ch. 9 Obsession .....................................................59

Ch. 10 Expectations ...............................................67

Ch. 11 The Wolf .....................................................74

Ch. 12 The Key to Each Other ................................81

Ch. 13 The Shift .....................................................89

Ch. 14 Hallucinations ............................................96

Ch. 15 Poison .......................................................102

Ch. 16 A Warning .................................................107

Ch. 17 Down a Grassy Hill....................................115

Ch. 18 Counsel from an Old Friend.......................122

Ch. 19 The Line....................................................129

Ch. 20 Aneira ......................................................136

Ch. 21 Bethel .......................................................143

Ch. 22 Killing ......................................................150

Ch. 23 The Difference ..........................................156

Ch. 24 The Edge of a Dark Forest.........................161

Ch. 25 Unwritten ................................................168

Ch. 26 Enchantments..............................................174
Ch. 27 The Path of the Wolf.................................181
Ch. 28 Incarnations ...............................................188
Ch. 29 A Villain......................................................194
Ch. 30 Strategizing ...............................................200
Ch. 31 For the Last Time......................................207
Ch. 32 The Signs ...................................................213
Ch. 33 A Puzzle Piece...........................................220

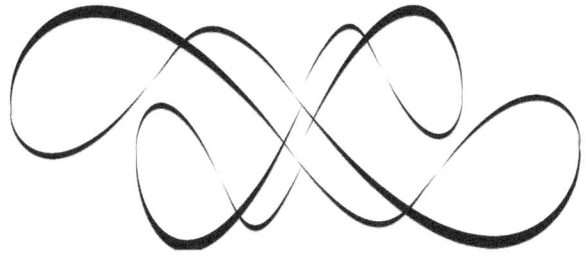

# Chapter 1

# ERIN HOLT

The city felt different, palpably different from what she was used to. As Erin breathed in deeply, inhaling the humid, moist air, all she could feel was a tantalizing curiosity. She couldn't help but wonder if this was what it felt like to be wicked? And if so, why did it beckon her so? Was this her true nature, craving, well craving something — something intangible and yet pervasive?

What an exhilarating feeling, being so completely out of one's element, both disorienting and, yes, admittedly, a bit intoxicating. But it was what she'd wanted for some time — to simply escape who she was.

It had been chance, sort of. She and her friend, Giselle, had enrolled in classes at an art education seminar at the convention center in New Orleans. It was a far cry from her home in Arkansas, Fayetteville, where she'd spent all her life. But this, this was meant to be a grand adventure for the two girls. Her parents, Gerald and Marion, had acquiesced with some trepidation. But they seemed to acknowledge that it was far past time to let go. After all, she was twenty-six, regardless of her delicate past.

She and Giselle had deliberately not booked a room in the Marriot near where the classes would be held but instead had gone off the beaten track, reserving a place for the week at a lovely little boutique hotel right in the heart of the French Quarter. The plan was to walk or ride a streetcar to the classes every morning after breakfast at a local eatery or pastry shop along the way. Well, that was the plan, but as it was, the best-laid plans—

Giselle came down with the flu. It was early November, quite chilly back home. It happened just a few days before the trip, catastrophic really. And the pressure began mounting for her to cancel as well. Her mother wanted to go with her, but that would entail quite an absence from her job. She'd been an elementary school teacher for over thirty years. This was the career path that Erin had intended to pursue as well, but then something, something within, had pulled her more in the artistic direction, so she compromised — art education, a field she was slowly obtaining a Master's degree in rather than getting a job right away.

But this trip, on this important trip, there was no one to accompany her. It would be a test. She had her own money. She'd saved it from selling her art, paintings and crafts, to local businesses in the city. Her mother did pressure her to cancel, and a few times she almost did, but something inside, something so strong, made her push through. On a level, she really needed this. Why exactly? Well, that part of the equation was elusive.

Erin laid back on the queen-sized bed at the Hotel St. Madeleine and continued to watch the ceiling fan take another meandering spin around its circumference. She'd arrived in New Orleans in the late afternoon, nearly an hour ago. Taking a shuttle from the airport, she collapsed on the bed after calling her parents and assuring them that all was well. It had been exhausting, being around so many people in the airport, the emotional goodbyes, and then the trip — getting onto an airplane for the first time, so many unknowns. It was draining.

Perhaps a nap and then later something to eat. It was Saturday, and the seminar wasn't starting until Monday. Two whole days for her and Giselle to explore the city. But there was no Giselle, just her, Erin Holt, alone on her grand adventure.

◆

The dream, this particular dream, took control powerfully, though it was undeniably familiar. It was warm, summery, and the sun was beating down on her bare arms, energizing. The grass beneath her was warm, alive. She breathed deeply, so much better to be outside where she could feel, feel everything. Her legs dangled into the edge of the creek as she rested on its bank. A thousand things rushed rampantly through her mind — thoughts, sensations, emotions dancing in, greedily taking up space so that she didn't hear, didn't hear the footsteps approaching her.

But she did hear the voice that was now perilously close. "Well, what do we have here?"

◆

Her eyes snapped open. The room came into sharp focus, but everything was alien. It came back in a rush. That's right, the Hotel St. Madeleine, New Orleans. The heavy sleep and confusion of the dream still clung to her as she sat up. Looking down at the thin black band around her slender wrist, it took her a moment to focus her eyes to read it. It was after midnight. How could she have slept that long?

Her head throbbed, and her stomach cramped. She hadn't eaten since that morning.

The sounds from the street below drifted upward. Her hearing was acute — people, people talking, music. Downstairs, the city was very much alive, even at this late hour.

She was the one who had wanted something different, out of her comfort zone. Steeling herself, she brushed out her long auburn hair in front of the mirror, then changed from her traveling clothes to a pair of blue jeans and an ivory-colored sweater accompanied by her signature short black boots. Erin was all about boots, particularly the powerful sound they made hitting the pavement. After all, sounds and textures were once all she had.

The weather was a bit warmer than back home, but it didn't matter. She could always push up her sleeves if need be. Adventure, adventure, she hummed the word in her mind like a mantra. Doing this gave her courage and the impetus not to admit that deep down she was hesitant, painfully insecure about so much.

She'd pulled her hair up into a loose bun, her wide hazel eyes staring back at her, trying to reassure her. She could wait, wait until the morning and not venture out on the streets at this late hour. That would be prudent. And if she dug around thoroughly enough, she might just find a package of crackers or mints stuffed somewhere in her purse or traveling bag. But that wouldn't be much of an adventure, and she was trying to shift the tone of her life.

The eyes stared back at her out of the reflection. Who exactly are you trying to convince? They demanded boldly.

Applying a bit of make-up, not enough to attract attention, but enough to enliven her hopelessly pale skin, she worked to settle her nerves. Erin wasn't really pretty. At least she didn't think so, though granted, her opinions on this topic were newly formed and always evolving. But from time to time, she could achieve striking, interesting contrasts. That was who she was — one filled with contrasts.

♦

The small restaurant within the Hotel St. Madeleine was closed, not a big surprise, given the hour. So, it quickly became apparent if she wanted something to eat, she would have to venture out onto the streets of the French Quarter. The sad truth was she couldn't remember the last time she was out this late at night.

She did, however, have good instincts, born of years of her mother's relentless coaching: *"Always pay attention to your feelings."* And she'd often tacked on, *"It's essential. It could be the only thing protecting you from potential disaster."*

With courage and caution, she stepped out of the doors of the St. Madeleine and onto the pavement of New Orleans' French Quarter. The humidity of the weather hit her at once, tangibly, on her skin. Here, it wasn't exactly cold or warm, somewhere stuck firmly between. Definitively, there was a different atmosphere, undeniably thicker, more crowded with impressions, sensation if there was such a thing. She likened it to being on a strange new planet, alien terrain that she was ill-adjusted to. Continuing to walk away from the hotel, distantly, she could hear music filtering down the brick-laden streets. With no predetermined direction in mind, she instinctually followed it.

Plenty of people were about as she rounded the corner of Chartres St., then slowly followed St. Louis up to the edge of Bourbon. So loud, the volume actually tangibly increased as she approached Bourbon Street.

In some ways, it felt safer amongst more people, but in other ways not. It crossed her mind more than once to return to the warm, cozy room of the St. Madeleine, but her stomach protested, aching with hunger.

So bizarre, everything around her felt like a party, a celebration of sorts. What a contagiously intoxicating atmosphere to be caught up in. There was much laughter, people milling in and out of the street and back into the open restaurants and clubs in droves. Oh yes, who was it who had told her — *"Just avoid Bour-*

*bon Street!"* A bad thing to suddenly remember; perhaps it was her uncle, and here she was, her little black boots hitting the sultry pavement of the very place she should avoid.

It crashed in on her suddenly how tired she was on so many levels — not just physically, but tired of being predictable, tired of fulfilling expectations.

She continued to walk, the hunger inside her subsiding as her eyes gobbled in the sights around her. It was dizzying as she soaked in the currents of wild sensation around her. She should step back and distance herself. That would be prudent, but then again, there was that pervasive feeling of having lived her life like a ship in a bottle. Indulging and maybe reveling a bit was too hard to resist.

As she meandered onward, intent on soaking up the atmosphere, Erin walked past a brightly lit, open tavern. It was not unique along the street. Back-to-back bars and restaurants with open French doors whose patrons spilled out onto the sidewalk were just about everywhere. But as she passed this one, just out the periphery of her vision, she noticed a group of young men standing outside, perhaps a bit younger than she. And almost immediately, as she passed by, they seemed to take notice of her. Holding beer bottles and looking a bit scruffy, she wouldn't be surprised if they'd been out there drinking for some time. She turned away, intent on pretending as though she hadn't noted their interest.

All she really wanted was to get something to eat, not engage anyone. But, then, as was her luck, one of them deliberately stepped out into the street, blocking her path. So abrupt and jarring, this reminded her now quite concretely of that intangible peril that she was warned to avoid.

The man, although she wanted to say boy, smiled at her in a creepy, slimy way. Quite clearly, he was feeling no pain. "How about I buy you a drink, beautiful?" He said as an internal alarm journeyed up her spine.

"No thanks," trying to deliberately walk around him. After all, it wasn't her first time brushing off undesired attention, but she usually didn't feel quite so vulnerable. And then, without warning, he reached out, roughly grabbing her arm. So jarring, his bruising touch felt like a hot scorch on her skin. It was true that Erin had always been painfully sensitive to contact. Yanking away in an abrupt reflex, she spun quickly to find a path away from him, away from the sick feeling that emanated from his contact.

"Hey," behind her, calling after her, but she fled, not quite running, but close enough to it. Her formerly hungry stomach now flipped with nausea. In just a split second, the grand adventure had been turned despairingly on its head.

She kept going, with no thought to direction, until finally, she forced herself to slow. Her breaths were panicked. It was foolish, amazingly foolish. She was alone in a strange city after midnight, so vulnerable. And then she just stopped, right there in the middle of the street because her feet refused to take her any further. Looking around with disorientation, it was clear if she went much further it would be too far away from her safe little room at the St Madeleine.

Glancing backward hesitantly, there was no sign of the drunken idiot in any kind of pursuit. He probably couldn't walk steady enough for that. Now, here was the dilemma. How was she going to get back to her hotel and avoid another nasty scene? The idea of getting something to eat had nearly been abandoned — too upset and too angry at herself for her stupidity. Yes, indeed, exactly how would she take on the world if she couldn't even handle an encounter with some drunken kid?

Maybe if she just walked back quickly, quickly past the bar where they may not even be now, if she just walked fast. But she was afraid. His touch, something about him, made her sick to the core. There must be another route back to the St. Madeleine. She would need to get directions, but she'd left her phone charging back at the hotel. It had been almost completely run down.

Despair and paralysis both battled for dominance as she stood simply in confusion in the middle of Bourbon St. She kept looking around frantically, foolishly, as though there might be an answer out there. Then, out of nowhere, something caught her eye, actually a someone — a man, standing on the other side of the street quietly watching her.

Now, she wasn't dumb enough to be stupid twice, given what had just happened. Turning away, she intended to continue walking, but she didn't. Instead, she turned and looked again. She couldn't seem to stop herself. He had his back against a building, silently observing her with his arms crossed. It was just a man, another reveler in the French Quarter, just a guy, blond, wearing a tan sports coat and dark pants.

She looked away. It was time to move on. She needed to, not wanting a repeat of what had just happened. What she wanted was to keep walking, keep walking, maybe find a restaurant, kill a little time, and then go back to the hotel. It was a plan. But her body wasn't moving. His eyes, his eyes were on her, on her back. She was certain of it. But oddly, it wasn't scary like the other. It felt like a pull, a gentle pull, though insistent, tugging at her to turn around again.

Erin breathed in deeply, resisting. Her life couldn't end here, not now, murdered by some maniac in New Orleans.

*"But did you know she was out prowling around Bourbon St. after midnight? That is not the Erin we knew."*

But did any of them really know Erin? Did she? Such irrelevant questions to be peppering herself with, standing in the middle of the street like this.

8

It was becoming strangely overwhelming, the impulse, so compelling, distracting. Again, she turned around — not planning it, not thinking about it, just letting it happen, returning his gaze.

Trembling somewhat, so emotional, so close to tears, what was she doing? Things had unraveled badly. And yet, he was there, calmly watching her.

Why?

Did he think he knew her? Maybe he'd mistaken her for someone else. She tried to place him. Maybe it would come to her. But no, it was brushed aside. She didn't know him, not at all.

And this was rude. No doubt of that, but her eyes were locked, staring back at him, rooted to this overly familiar spot in the middle of Bourbon Street. Everything around, all the noise, the cacophony of mixing music from different establishments, the people walking or stumbling by, all of it just slipped away. And there was only this, this cord now connecting his gaze to hers.

*"Yes, Erin just disappeared one night on the streets of that awful city. No one has seen or heard of her since."*

All those whispers of caution and doom continued to float around, somewhat disconnected. But it changed nothing. And after an indeterminable stretch of time, he began to move, to walk towards her. She was sure in those moments she didn't breathe, but nor did she pass out unconscious from lack of air.

And he stopped walking just in front of her.

Well, she had wanted an adventure. *Be careful what you wish for.*

His eyes, unquestionably familiar, rang a distant bell but refused to link to anything tangible.

"I—" She started to speak but then dropped the idea of conversation. What should she say? She must seem ridiculous, but there was no escape from that now.

The man, the blond man in front of her wasn't smiling, though he had a pleasant face. He actually looked quite serious, as though something weighed on him. Her mind searched frantically for possible explanations, but no, coherency had left the building.

And then he spoke, "What do you need?" a rich voice, warm and comforting like her room up at the Hotel St. Madeleine. It had a wonderful tone, and she had always prided herself on being a connoisseur of voices. But then again, some distant paranoid whisper asked if serial killers possessed such voices.

What had he said? Oh yes, and why had he said that? She took a deep breath, deciding to keep things superficial. Perhaps, then she could extricate herself from whatever this was in one piece. "Oh, I was just going to get something to eat but got a bit lost, I think."

A slight smile touched his lips fleetingly. "Then come along with me," he answered, somewhat jarring and enticing in the same breath. An invitation, she must say *No*. It was prudent. But that *No*, didn't seem to want to come out. Everything had such an unreal texture — this night, this city, and now there was this man with whom she felt no alarm, no sense of danger whatsoever.

"I can't," she murmured because she had to, not particularly because she wanted to.

He looked at her calmly as though the answer was not so unexpected. "Just a café a half a block down, quite public."

"On this street?" she asked a bit anxiously.

"Unfortunately," he replied with the barest hint of amusement.

10

He was relaxing her, having no idea why. Her well-trusted inner radar seemed to be on the blink, telling her that she was safe when she knew that to be highly improbable. But still, she hesitated. It didn't feel safe, not so much this man but around them. The inky, sultry blackness of the night was overwhelming. "We won't stay long," he said, almost as though in answer to her concerns.

Another breath, not as deep, as she tried to remember something, an elusive thing, nagging at her that seemed to want to melt away in the shadows. "All right," she replied, and they began to walk. "I don't even know your name," she murmured, trying desperately to establish some normalcy in this disquieting situation.

"It's Ethan, Ethan Garraint." And she wondered vaguely why he hadn't asked for hers.

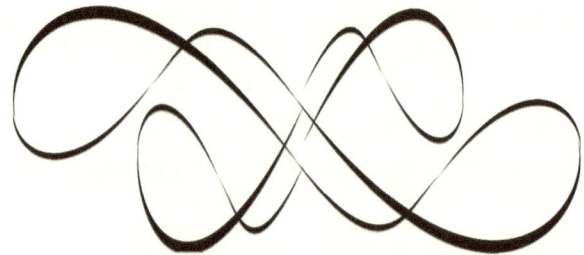

# Chapter 2

# Unexpected

So many of the restaurants seemed connected to the street itself, with French doors wide open and balconies and patios situated out on the pavement — not like at home, where things felt more separated.

"How's the salad?" he asked. She glanced up. He wasn't eating, just drinking a beer and keeping her company. She'd given him her name, not because he asked, but because it felt rude and oddly uncomfortable not to. After all, she had to keep this somehow tethered to what felt normal. And it was normal for strangers sharing a meal of sorts to exchange names and information about each other. So, she did, and here she was, casually drinking a glass of wine with her shrimp salad.

"It's good," she answered in earnest. They were sitting at a small wrought iron table out on a balcony, so much easier to see the street below with a slight bit of distance. It was more comfortable, and she was undeniably calmer. Below them, she could see people, even more people than before milling about. "It only seems to get busier here," she murmured.

"It's the weekend," he said softly. Ethan, her companion Ethan Garraint, enunciated in a unique way when he spoke as though there was some vestige of an accent clinging to his speech. For most of her life, she'd listened so closely to voices that she could pick up nuances others might not focus on.

Erin leaned back, sipping her wine. An unexpected peacefulness was settling over her that she had no idea if she'd really earned. Had the peril she'd felt descending not so long ago passed? Or was she fooling herself? But admittedly all seemed better now, everything not so threatening. She focused on the man across from her, who seemed content to rest easily in their long silences. "I appreciate your rescue," she said. "But I have to admit I'm not so sure why you did it."

His gaze returned to her. He hadn't spoken a great deal since they'd first met, just small things, seeing to her comfort. At first, she'd thought he seemed troubled, caught up in some concerns well beyond them, but then it did seem to ease a bit. "Well, rescuing a beautiful woman always seems like a worthy endeavor," he said smoothly, with enough humor that made it sound quite natural. And again, it hit her, that nagging, bothering feeling as though there was something to do, something she'd forgotten. "Do you like the city, Erin Holt?"

She smiled, couldn't help it, and her heart unconsciously picked up its beat at his use of her name and the realization that only seconds ago he'd called her beautiful. He was attractive and charming, innately charming, but not at all artificial, simply just something very easy and natural woven into his nature. "I honestly don't know. I haven't been here very long. Being out here tonight is my first exposure to it."

"That's a pity," he commented, lifting the frosty glass schooner of beer to his lips. "It can be quite a remarkable place, filled with history, atmosphere, but nighttime — let's just say it brings out many layers. I wouldn't base your evaluation solely on this first impression."

13

She nodded slowly, continuing to enjoy the moment, and let her guard down. "I'm trying to hold back on judgments. I really just wanted to see something new."

He looked at her with an undefinable sort of warmth in his expression. "You're a long way from home. Aren't you Erin?" Such an odd observation and a little jolting, she had no idea how to answer. The comment had caught her strangely. It felt laced with intangible things that only made her feel more confused. "I don't know. I suppose." Again, he just seemed to be staring at her, making her feel as if he was expecting something. "I was supposed to be traveling with a friend, but—" she stopped, feeling incredibly awkward, "then things changed."

She closed her eyes for a second, just for a second, reminding herself of a world she used to live in long ago, then slowly opened them again. "I think I need to get back," she nearly whispered.

He didn't question but just replied. "All right."

◆

They walked largely in silence back down Bourbon Street. Although the environment on the surface had not changed a bit, it did feel different this time. The uncertainty, the feeling of vulnerability, and the encroaching danger did not close in as they had before. And she knew without a scrap of external evidence that the change was because of her companion.

As they passed the bar called the Blacksmith's Pub, where she'd had that nasty encounter with the drunken man, a tremor of panic passed through her as she saw him and his group still outside. Erin could actually feel it on her skin the moment he spotted her again, but then, quite suddenly, his eyes focused on the man next to her.

So strange, how some confrontations can occur without a sound and without even an action. But it was tangible, through the thickness of the air, a crackle in the atmosphere, and then her aggressor from earlier in the evening looked away.

14

Her heart clutched a bit at the realization. He'd frightened him. This Ethan Garraint, the man escorting her back to her hotel, had somehow frightened that boy away without a word. Clearly, he was perceived as a threat, although she couldn't feel this at all.

Erin, who did pride herself on being a bit of an intellectual, sent her mind back to quickly review what she knew about him. He'd said he was a craftsman, built furniture. He sported a short beard and well-trimmed mustache, hair was ash blond, eyes bluish-gray, around six feet, she estimated roughly, not overly muscular but trim. His demeanor fluctuated, pleasant, charming in a removed sort of way, and yes, that accent thing. It wasn't something she should focus on too closely, as she knew her speech was often laced with tinges of a southern Arkansas inflection. But his speech and choice of words intrigued her so. She'd thought it was French, but it was nearly indistinguishable, European surely.

And then there were her instincts. She had cultivated a sort of internal alarm to pick up a sense of danger when it was near. It was a gift of sorts, left over from the old days. Her other senses had developed more keenly due to her lack of—

"How long?" he interrupted her thoughts, asking as they turned the corner off of Bourbon Street.

"What?" She said a bit startled.

"Sorry, how long did you say you'd be in town?"

She must be calm, all this analyzing only had served to work her up into a near panic. "I fly out Friday."

"Six days," he murmured lightly. "What miracles can be wrought in six days?"

✦

As they slowly meandered up to the front of the Hotel St. Madeleine, it suddenly became somewhat obvious, even to Erin, that her new companion might be intent on escorting her to her room. He held the door as she walked into the lobby and then stepped into the elevator beside her as it began to ascend to the third floor. More startling than the fact that he was with her was the fact that she hadn't stopped him. Why hadn't she? First, at the front of the hotel, saying a quick, curt *"Thank you and good-night."* Then, barring that, at least at the elevator, but she didn't. She was silent and complacent, not even meeting his eyes. But instead, simply feeling his presence, actually sensing the heat emanating from his body.

It was confusing, so confusing — this alien, hypnotic sort of lull she was moving through. This wasn't her, certainly not what she expected herself to be.

And she reminded herself emphatically that he was a stranger, a fact that she needed to remember. This Ethan Garraint was unquestionably a total stranger.

It was confusing, how to handle things because there was the pull, the odd, inexplicable draw to the man beside her.

They stepped out of the elevator, and without a word, she began to walk toward her room. He was following behind her, and she knew now it was time to end things.

Admittedly, Erin didn't have much experience with men. There hadn't been much time for that with everything else. So, she wasn't adept at navigating such unknown waters. As they arrived in front of her hotel room, she stopped and slowly turned around. She was flustered, her face warm, and he, well, he was just standing there with little expression, quietly watching her. "Thank you for the dinner and the rescue," she began a bit shakily.

But almost just as she'd begun speaking, quite seamlessly Ethan Garraint had moved closer, holding a single finger to her lips as though to silence her. It was beyond unexpected, catching her completely off guard, as did his next move when he leaned in and pulled her fully into his arms. The movement was so fluid and yet aggressive that even before she had a chance to think, to understand what was happening, he had begun kissing her.

Shocking, she had expected something, but not this, not this. In reflex, she tried to pull away but could feel the steely strength in his arms. Then, on its heels, something else happened. That magnetic pull that had been insidiously present ever since she'd laid eyes on him exploded with this contact, powerfully seeping into her, draping itself over her. Without thought, without the ability not to, she simply let go, surrendered perhaps was a better term. As he kissed her with increasing passion, she found herself kissing him back. A thousand sensations flooded across her senses as she ceased thinking at all.

Then suddenly, he stopped, and she found herself only beginning to surface from a mesmerizing haze. In that moment, she said what she felt she should, so shakily, "I can't do this."

And again, he pulled her closer, reminding her of the magnetic pull of his very skin. Simply whispering into her ear. "Give me the key."

And she did.

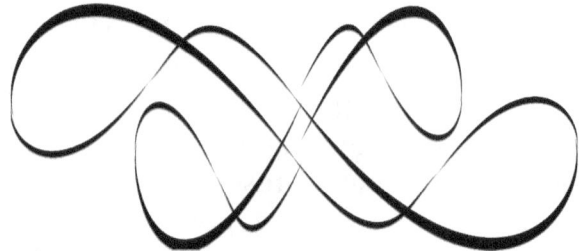

# Chapter 3

# DARKNESS

"What is darkness?"

There was silence, although she was certain that she had sent the question out quite succinctly.

*"Your question is layered. Of what precisely do you refer?"*

A frustration emanated from someplace deep within her core. She wasn't old at that point, just a teenager, just thirteen, perhaps, or even a bit younger. And without sight, for her, it seemed an obvious question, not layered at all. "It's simple. I have no vision, and people around me tell me that I live in darkness. I want to understand what they mean." There was a forthrightness in the question, a determination. It was the way she navigated her world, lacking tentativeness and hesitation.

He was near. She could actually hear him, maybe feel him, but not in the same way she would feel her mother's hands or her arms as she reached out to her. She knew touch. She would run her fingertips along surfaces and feel textures, forms, smooth, rough with bumpy edges, warmth, or chill.

*"Your eyes, you can feel them with your hands."*

"Of course, although only lightly, it's painful."

*"Yes. The vision you lack emanates from there."*

"I know that. I'm not stupid."

She felt his soft laughter rather than heard it as though it were tucked away somewhere inside of her. *"This concept of darkness is simply an opposite — the absence of sight becomes darkness."*

"But I see colors, light, visions. It's not darkness, although I'm told it's only my imaginings, memories from before I lost my vision. I'm told what I do not have."

There was silence, though she could feel him thinking. If she dreamed, she would see him differently, separate, not so close to her own thoughts. *"Do you believe that this is only your imaginings?"*

The silence enveloped her as she considered. "No, I do not."

And once again, she felt the laughter and then quietly, *"Good girl."*

♦

Erin Holt had lost her eyesight at age five, a car accident, blunt trauma to the head, and hemorrhaging that took her vision.

From a very young age, sound was her guide to an outside world that she could touch occasionally but also seemed quite disconnected from. But there were other things, the whispers she heard that should have been inaudible — the sadness of a mother who felt guilt and despair for her only daughter and the determination of a father who wanted her to be as normal a child as possible.

It was true. From early on, she was told quite often that she lived in darkness.

19

What exactly qualified as darkness, she wasn't at all sure. Because she did see, she saw color and visions, structures at times, perhaps places. Behind her sightless eyes was another world, yes, separate from the one her family spoke to her from, but it did have its inhabitants.

♦

It was a garden, a lush garden with roses climbing up a white metal trellis. She breathed in deeply, the perfume of the air. This, of course, was a dream or perhaps a vision. From time to time, the two got mixed up. But this one occurred when she was only fifteen.

"Hello, Enid."

He leaned against a tree, a tall, fair-haired fellow. He was dressed in black, black shirt and black pants, quite stark against his vivid background. The colors and designations came to her easily in dreams, although they were forgotten later.

"That's not my name." She said pointedly. Back then, it was her way to be direct.

Shrugging, "It's how I know you." He watched her from that leaning position of his up against the tree. It was not so unusual for her to see people in her dreams. She still had memories from when she had sight. But those from the dreams felt new, different, as though from another realm.

"This isn't real," she pronounced.

"It is a dream," he replied, "but that doesn't mean it isn't real." He had a rich voice, smooth but deep, kind of reminded her of the taste of hot caramel.

She looked down beneath her. It was a stone bench she was sitting on. At first, as she ran her hands along it, she had thought granite. She had touched smooth granite before. But the texture was wrong. This was more polished, slick, and so cool to the touch. She ran her hand over its smooth surface. "What is this?"

"Onyx," he replied softly.

She'd felt the onyx in her hands, but that was only a small stone. This felt quite powerful, emanating vibrations that made her skin tingle.

"That seems curious for a bench to be made of onyx," she murmured.

He smiled, and it lit something familiar in her chest, right around her heart. "It's a dream, my Lady. The sky is the limit in a dream."

He'd straightened up from the tree but still had moved no closer to her. "We have met before?"

"Many times — don't you remember?" He said lightly.

She shook her head. She didn't remember, although there had been voices, one particular voice so often in her mind. "I'm not sure. Where is this dream going? I mean, what am I supposed to do here?"

Another smile, he liked her. She could feel that from him. "Nothing to do, just be."

♦

Of course, he was part of her imagination. She told herself that, and occasionally, he told her that as well.

"So, you're like an imaginary friend."

"Yes, a friend."

"But what will I call you?"

"Geraint will do."

He would come to her in whispers at times, and she would feel his presence as clearly as if someone had walked into the room. But then, this would dissipate, leaving her wondering if indeed he was real at all.

"The name Enid, where does it come from?"

"The past."

"And Geraint?"

They were walking outside, outside a magnificent castle in the mountains. It looked like it was constructed of white marble, glistening in the sun. "Is it so important for you to categorize everything?"

"I'm trying to understand."

He laughed a bit, amused, she guessed, as they continued to walk around the well-paved pathway. "Very well, as you wish."

"Even an imagination must be built upon something. I've read the Arthurian stories, those names, the stories, in brail of course."

"They have indeed become stories, more fiction than fact now."

"But they were based on something."

"Lost truths," he murmured, seeming reluctant to give her anything very concrete.

"And you are tied to this Geraint?"

"I thought I was simply your imagining."

"I don't think I believe that."

"Well then, of course, you must follow your own mind."

◆

Geraint became a confidante, an advisor, a guide through her perilous world. And then, when she reached twenty, well, everything changed.

The first thing she remembered seeing was the light, painful, burning light when the doctor removed the protective guards from her eyes. It felt like being born, or so she imagined, being thrust from a somewhat warm, familiar cocoon of a world into a harsh, cold, unfamiliar terrain.

It was a miracle, in some respects, a vitrectomy, a procedure that removes the jellylike tissue behind the eye's lens and replaces it with a saline solution, ostensibly undoing the damage that the hemorrhaging had caused.

Yes, truly a miracle, but a traumatic one just the same.

"Oh God," she'd rasped, over and over again. Even she could hear the raw panic in her voice.

Her mother's hands were on her shoulders, trying to hold her still.

Then, Dr. Peterson explaining, "I know it must be overwhelming, my dear."

They misinterpreted, of course, believing she was happy. She wasn't happy, excited, horrified, or much of anything. It was such a shock. A complete and jarring change, a disconnect from how she'd lived before.

Always, she'd relied on other senses, and now the world expected her to rely on her vision –– imperfect, flawed vision that would never truly see the world as deep down she knew it to be.

It was a terribly tumultuous time, one that someone who had not lived as she had could ever understand. In many ways, her world, the one she'd learned from her childhood, simply slipped away to be replaced by a hard, structured existence that Erin now found necessary to conform to.

Of course, at first, she was so busy that she didn't realize at all what had disappeared — what she'd lost.

At night, Erin would still dream and sometimes almost catch glimpses of her companion, but then he was gone. He simply slipped away from her, forcing her to accept the fact that she had simply created him for comfort.

◆

The impact hit her rather abruptly. How could she do this? How could she allow this stranger to take her into her hotel room? It was insane. It was so dangerous, and she felt absolutely power-less to stop it.

Ethan Garraint had taken the key card out of her hand and opened the door but waited, waited for her to step across the threshold.

But then he'd held his hand out to her. "It's all right," he said reassuringly.

And for some unknown reason, she'd reached out shakily and took it, feeling acutely as though something else had taken hold of her, something unconscious that wasn't listening at all to her mind. And then they were inside, and the door was closed behind them.

Again, she tried to get out protestations, "Look, I'm sorry if I gave you the wrong impression. You're a stranger to me and I simply can't—"

He dropped the key card on the dresser beside the door and then abruptly put his hands on the sides of her face. "Look at me. Look at me, Erin. Now, am I really a stranger?" His voice sounded deep now, rough in her ears, nearly akin to a low growl of some sort.

His eyes stared into hers, that blue-gray color, intense but also kind. And then something happened, inexplicable, in a whirlwind, her breath caught in her throat as images suddenly came rushing back in, the garden, long walks by the castle, whispers — so many crashing in. It was not possible. "Oh God," she whispered in complete disbelief.

"I've been waiting a long time for you, Enid, to come home."

And then he was kissing her again, her utter confusion becoming drowned in the passion he seemed able to elicit from her at will.

"Don't be afraid of me," he said huskily, effortlessly sweeping her into his arms, carrying her to that queen-sized bed.

"You're not real," she whispered as he almost gingerly laid her down on the mattress.

"No, you've just forgotten," he said, covering her mouth with his again.

Her head was swirling in the sensation. How could she let this happen? But she was, she was letting him kiss her, touch her, letting him remove her clothes. He would be her first lover, a man from her dreams she'd only known as Geraint.

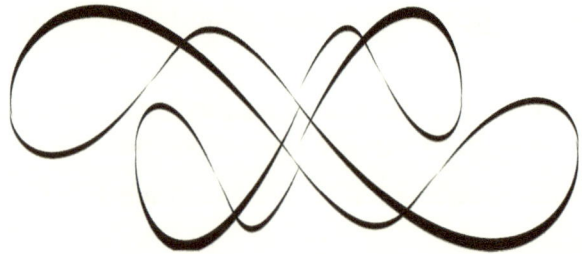

# Chapter 4

# BEFORE

He steeled himself. From where he stood, at least a block away, he saw the dark-haired man grab her. It took everything inside him to stop from leaping across the short distance and ripping his arm out of its socket. But he wasn't in wolf form, although for a moment, it absolutely felt as though he was, so strong was his desire to protect her.

In merely seconds, she'd yanked away and was moving quickly from the cretin. He leaned against the brick building, bowing his head momentarily just to calm himself. These emotions, uncontrollable elemental emotions that came with being in her proximity, had to be pushed down. It was just like the early days when he first became the lycanthrope. He had no control back then. Once the animal was released, his mind would simply sink into its impulses.

◆

*A Good Man*

*Am I a good man? It's a question that I've pondered from time to time. Sometimes, I even question if I am a man at all, given the unnatural state of my life. But then again, I'm reminded and indeed humbled by the fact that I do have a man's weaknesses, passions, needs, and, yes, emotions. Much as I'd like to hold myself separate, as it would be more convenient, whatever greater supreme being is out there occasionally brings me to my knees and reminds me of all those frailties.*

*I am not an arrogant man, though I would admit I used to be. I was heartily convinced at one time that I could bend life quite adeptly to the force of my will.*

*I was a fighter, a soldier, someone who let too many victories cloud his judgment. When you come home a hero, it's wise not to believe what everyone says of you. It imbues you with a false sense of self-importance.*

*And that is where the humbling comes in.*

♦

## 1243 – The Languedoc region in southern France

"Wolves mate for life."

He looked up in amusement at the elder. Well, in physical age, at least, Brother Guidrade appeared a good forty years older than him. He wore a full white beard and did walk with a staff and, in appearance, seemed to have quite a bit of seniority to Etienne, the name that Ethan Garraint was known by so long ago when he'd entered the service of the Cathars of Southern France as a mercenary. But as was the nature of things, he had learned here and from the long course of many years on this earth that appearances did not always reflect the truth.

He laughed, leaning back against one of the inner castle walls of Montségur, taking a long drink from a flask of water. "So, I've heard. But what brings this random observation to mind?"

The old man, as he liked to refer to him in his mind, looked at him with all seriousness. This had been his way when he had some profound wisdom to impart to his pupil. "I think you understand where I am heading with this."

Etienne closed his eyes for a moment. They never really talked about it, the Cathar people whom he had settled with. He felt it in his skin, in his blood, that somehow, with their deep spiritual connection to the earth, they had gleaned his true lycanthropic nature. But if this indeed was true, it was as if they had stepped back and respected his privacy. "Perhaps you should just come out with it."

"There was a woman once for you, Etienne."

His eyes widened with surprise. No, he hadn't expected this. "Yes, a long time ago."

Guidrade nodded. "Someone very special to you that I think perhaps you still mourn."

It was true. Etienne felt a profound stab in his heart at the very mention of her. It was a wound he tried to bury but never really seemed to leave. "She was my wife."

"And she left you."

He took another mouthful of water. "Not of her free will, but yes, most do," he said rather flatly.

"I understand. But, in all the time afterward, you've found no one to replace her."

"No" he murmured gruffly, "it's not possible."

"And that is my point. Between you and this one woman, there was a link, a spiritual link. It is a sacred bond that nothing can be substituted for."

He straightened up, his back chafing a bit from resting against the rough stone of the castle balustrade. "I don't understand what you are trying to say with all of this." He was, after all,

28

not the most patient man at the time, nor did he encourage sharing private details of his life.

"The Perfects here, you've noticed many choose celibacy."

"Yes," he mumbled, "I assumed it was just part of your religion."

"Some but not all choose it."

That was true, although he'd never spent any time considering this. "Yes, Sister Bruna and her husband Arnaud."

"Yes, and others, they seek a union with their match, their spiritual match. It is a powerful thing when two spirits are joined in communion, who have such a connection. Was it this way with your wife?"

Etienne took a quick breath, then for only a moment, allowed the distant memories to rush into the present. It was a time he usually endeavored to block from his conscious mind, so painful was the loss. But just for an instant, he allowed himself to see her watching him with wide, dark eyes, her face filled with curiosity and some trepidation. She'd sensed it before he had understood — the power he would have over her and the power she would hold over him. "Yes, I remember. It was overwhelming. I'd never felt anything like it. Without shocking you, Brother Guidrade, I knew the moment I saw her that I had to have her."

The old man laughed beside him softly, "Carnally?"

"Yes, although I did marry her."

"The need for connection is powerful. The spirit responds and is affected, perhaps even transformed by the physical. Remember the melding, body, mind, spirit. The spirits created for each other are tied to each other's energy. They become more together than separate. It is a sacred thing. That is why so many of the Perfects are celibate. They understand that union with a spirit who is not their proper match could be as detrimental as the reverse is positive. Can you understand this?"

29

"I suppose. But many in the world follow their carnal appetites as a recreational vocation."

"Yes, to their own damage, spiritual damage is a subtle thing, a slow erosion most aren't aware of until it's too late."

"I see," he replied, his mind slowly connecting these teachings to his own experience. It had been that way with her, a humbling, crushing realization that he needed her — was not just the fierce, solitary man that he had always felt himself to be.

"For you, being who you are, Etienne, energy is a powerful component of your life. You draw your energy from the earth. It sustains you. You must be aware and cognizant of every aspect of it. And there is something else."

"Yes Brother, what is it?"

"The one you are bonded with will return to the earth one day. Her spirit will reincarnate. And when that happens, it will be as it was before, a powerful, uncontrollable draw to you and you to her."

He didn't quite accept this concept of reincarnation that the Cathari seemed to embrace. And the thought of his once-beloved clothed in another flesh, another life, seemed more than a bit incomprehensible to him. "How do you know this, Brother Guidrade?"

"It has been seen and felt."

♦

The conversation had been long ago at the Castle of Montségur, perhaps only a year before Pope Innocent III led the genocide of the Cathar people during the Albigensian Crusade. It was so long ago, but the wisdom he gained from the blessed people still resonated with him. They had given him the strength to go on, to find purpose in an existence so unnatural, so protracted at times that it felt indeed to be simply an aberration.

It was so long ago, but even then, he'd already been alive for centuries. His was a life that began long ago in a distant land. In the beginning, he was a person he scarcely recognized now, young, headstrong, determined, and yes, stupid. Looking back now through eyes that had lived too long and seen too much of the world and the hearts of men, he wondered with some indulgence how he had survived as long as he did in those days without calamity — and why she'd looked twice at him.

Ethan breathed in deeply, a particular pain lodged just around his heart area. "Leave it alone" — wise voices drifted in, ones he couldn't put a name to just now. The city isn't safe, not for him, not for anyone connected to him. He wasn't convinced the threat of Claude Barraud had truly disappeared. That was why he'd lingered in the area instead of moving on.

He had to be sure, so he'd waited, waited for almost a year now, living quietly, laying a foundation for the next move in his journey overseas. It had been some time, but he'd decided to return to France, not the land of his birth, but perhaps the land of his rebirth. It would always be a significant place to him where he'd learned and, under the tutelage of the Cathari, had turned his life around. *Always give yourself something to look forward to.* Who'd told him that? It was something he did practice but just at this moment, he'd forgotten who exactly had given him that particular advice.

Ethan breathed in deeply, trying to clear his mind of the cobwebs of the past. The best-laid plans, he murmured aloud to himself, sipping a glass of scotch he'd poured half an hour before but had scarcely touched. His eyes glanced at a clock on the wall. He wondered what she was doing now, her first night in the city. All he had to do was stay put and do nothing. But there was that awareness, that pesky awareness skimming along his skin. Do nothing, soldier, just do nothing — easier said than done.

Chapter 5

# ETHAN

T he Quarter was active this night, with all sorts, all manner of people in its streets. He felt much, strange emanations generating from its eclectic group of inhabitants. He allowed himself to sink further into instinct and to prowl. He didn't know what had brought her to the city but doubted she would be here long.

He had already been roaming the area for several hours. More than once, he'd passed in front of the Hotel St. Madeleine, feeling her presence and fighting the inclination to pay her an unexpected visit. But he'd resisted. And as midnight approached, he thought it unlikely she'd be emerging tonight. He'd started to leave but then didn't. One more pass around the area wouldn't hurt.

If he intended to stay away from her, he could keep his distance while she was here. He could certainly manage this. And he tried not to allow himself to consider if that was what he truly wished. So long ago, when he married her, he was a man. He was no longer a man and so could not indulge in the desires of one.

And then he'd felt it. She was moving. He was several blocks away from the St. Madeleine when he detected the change. Strange how he could feel her energy as acutely as though he carried a specific radar for it. There was no way he could reach her inconspicuously where she was, so he decided on the other option — to subtly try to influence her to come to him.

He closed his eyes and focused on her, on her emotions, her thoughts. He breathed in deeply. Doing this was not devoid of its dangers. What he felt was familiar, and yet not. Living with her for many years, her energy, the textures of her soul, had become so very recognizable for him even though at the time he was untrained in matters of energy or psychic emanations. But what he felt from the woman whose body now carried his wife's spirit was a mixture of the old and the new, the core the same while the outward personality, the mind, the physical rhythm different, unique.

He strove to concentrate, gently enticing her to follow a certain path without being aware she was being influenced. He breathed deeply. There were so many other disruptive energies in this area. It was difficult. But he could feel it, feel her finally moving in his direction.

So, he waited quietly until he caught sight of her. And then, she was accosted by the man, the man his impulse was to shred. Once he opened his eyes again, he realized how close she was to him, only yards away, standing in the middle of the street. He could feel her fear, her panic from the encounter he'd just witnessed. His eyes were locked on her, but she hadn't seen him. He hadn't wanted her to. He hesitated, breathing deeply.

*"Are you some sort of mystical creature, my Lady?"*

*"I'm as real as you are."*

He waited, allowing her to make the choice. Either she would see him here, or she would move on, and he would release her forever.

Ethan waited calmly, relinquishing control of his destiny to fate in a way he couldn't remember having done for hundreds of years.

The girl turned around, her back facing him, and he felt she would walk away. But then, unexpectedly, she turned again and met his eyes. A jolt of recognition passed through him that he remembered from long ago. For a moment, she glanced down, but then again, her gaze returned to him. She saw him, and without thought, he moved toward her.

◆

Erin Holt was deeply shaken and seemed confused. The two emotions permeated her as he approached. In choosing this course, Ethan stopped thinking, stopped plotting and strategizing, and allowed himself to be guided solely by instinct. He wasn't foolish enough to think that cold reason could rule him now. Nothing about this present situation was in any way cold.

Her wide green eyes were filled with fear, so vulnerable, lost in a way that felt painful to him. This wasn't what he wanted for her, not at all.

She started to speak to him but stopped.

"What do you need?" was the only coherent thing he could manage to get out. This was monumentally more difficult than he had imagined. Here he was, standing across from her in the flesh, the girl he'd stood beside and supported through her blindness, and the woman, the echo of the woman he'd loved so long ago, more than anything and had lost.

They stood there in the midst of that chaotic street, and for a few moments, it was as though they were the only two people alive in the world, so intense was this contact. Then, somehow, inexplicably, life began to move again, and she answered him hesitantly. "I was just going to get something to eat but got a bit lost, I think."

He breathed in deeply, feeling the currents around him. He couldn't leave her. He could feel so much. She was extraordinary, brimming with powerful energy that would stand out like a beacon and draw those who wished to feed like parasites. He couldn't leave her alone. It was too dangerous.

But he must allay her fears, "Then come along with me," he said, adding smoothly, "Just a café a half a block down, quite public."

For a few moments, he thought she would refuse him. There was debating going on, but beyond that, beyond the surface, he knew that she felt it as well and was intrigued. It pleased him. His wife had a streak about her, a wildness that was drawn to him. Perhaps that was not entirely gone.

They walked largely in silence along the busy street although some minimal conversation flowed. Mostly, he took the time to learn about her, to learn more about the woman he didn't know.

He remembered her from before, her long dark red hair and large eyes, although unseeing. Now, they seemed even wider to him, perhaps intent on absorbing all she'd missed in her early years. He'd forgotten how preoccupied normal people were about time. But then, of course, for them, it was such a finite commodity.

"I didn't realize it would be like this," she murmured.

"What? The city?"

"Yes, I suppose. I don't know. It feels like so much is going on constantly."

"Well, the French Quarter has always been an area of concentrated living. So many cultures have been here and, in most ways, still are. I think you'll find it's unique to almost any other place in the world."

"Even Europe?" she said quietly.

"No, I think perhaps you're right in that. Places in Europe might well be the exception."

It was an odd conversation, not really comments between people who had just met. But then again, he did not expect anything ordinary between them.

Dinner was more of the same. He'd selected a restaurant whose second-floor patio balcony stretched over the busy street below. At least for a little while, it would give them some isolation from the chaotic world around them. From time to time, Erin would meet his eyes, and he knew she was trying to remember, trying to remember why their acquaintance felt like an easy one, why his presence felt familiar. He had worked to dissipate the recollections in her memory, but something within her, he suspected, resisted.

"Designing, building furniture, that seems like an unusual occupation," she said, sipping her wine.

"In some ways, I think it's a dying art, crafting and molding with your hands. Long ago, such artisans were revered, but now. Well, I suppose I'm a dinosaur."

"I doubt that. I mean, before I gained my sight, I spent so much time using my hands, learning from touch that I could feel differences in different types of stone and wood. They all have their unique properties. I suspect in what you do that—"

"That I would feel the same sorts of things?" She frowned a bit. She'd told him about regaining her sight. It felt like an odd confidence to tell a stranger, but then again, they were anything but that. And now, clearly, she was afraid that she'd overstepped. It was difficult to navigate these shifting boundaries between them. "Every living thing or thing that once had some sort of life has their presence, energy if you will."

She nodded, "Yes, that's what I meant."

"And for me, in building, I have to find one that will perfectly conform to its purpose."

Again, she nodded in understanding, then fell silent.

They'd crossed into strange territory. There was too much between them to express. And Erin Holt was frightened. Not exactly of him, but possibly of what was changing inside her because of him.

He wasn't at all surprised when she asked to leave. He'd expected it. He'd expected it the moment she'd agreed to accompany him. But now, he needed to decide where things would go.

He walked her back through the busy streets to her hotel. Again, they passed the man who had accosted her earlier, and he felt the rage rise up in him as he made eye contact. Immediately, he sensed that Erin had picked up on this. She was so sensitive. He remembered her gifts from before, gifts he had no idea if she'd carried with her into this lifetime. Would there be time for him to find out? He wondered.

As they entered the lobby of her hotel, his head began to drum with a slow throb. It wasn't exactly a headache. It was something else. His blood had become heated, not unlike when he had mutated into the wolf and would be on the hunt. He would feel the very rhythm of his blood throughout his body guiding him, taking over, drowning out conscious reason.

There were things to think about, decisions to be made. But he followed Erin into the elevator. Her eyes seemed a bit anxious, and she would not meet his gaze directly. He was making her nervous, and she wondered what he intended — something he was wondering himself.

When they reached her room, she began to say goodnight. But he stopped her. He didn't think. Ethan Garraint couldn't think anymore. It seemed this decision had been made long, long ago, deep in a forest on a summer's day.

Chapter 6

# AFTERMATH

S he opened her eyes.

The dream, or rather memory, lingered over her mind. There had been so many conversations and interactions that now felt new again, although they were from her past, a past until several hours ago she had not remembered.

The ceiling fan over the queen-sized bed spun slowly. There was a chill in the shadowed room. She pulled the covers over her bare skin and glanced to the side of her. The bed was empty.

She hesitated. Had she dreamed it all? Everything on this night had an unreal quality to it. But she chased away that thought. No, it was real. She had just slept with a man that she had known for perhaps only an hour. And then she sighed deeply, not altogether true. If she were to believe him, and now her recollections, she had known him for more than a decade before, although granted not a traditional acquaintance.

She sat up in the bed and noticed for the first time that the door leading out onto the small patio was open. And his sportscoat lay draped across the wicker chair poised near that door. Well, he wasn't gone, just taking in the night air.

She clutched the sheets and bedspread a little closer. She could barely soak in what had happened. An adventure? Yes, some might term it as such. It was bizarre, almost as though a hypnotic mesmerism had covered them, a spell woven around them both.

Pure sensation and pure need had taken over, and in truth, she did not feel at all like the same person she had been before in the lobby, in the elevator, in the hallway. Now she was someone else, someone new or perhaps not, just someone buried beneath the restrictions her life had clamped down on her. But whatever the case, this connection to this man, to Ethan or Geraint, or whoever he truly was, seemed as natural as breathing.

She allowed her feelings to stretch outward in a way that felt at odds with how she'd lived for so long. She could feel him, tangibly, out there on the balcony. In truth, he was virtually a stranger to her, her mind repeated like a mantra. Repeated so that, in some respect, she would be convinced, no matter how she truly felt. Perhaps she should flee. Perhaps that would be the smartest thing to do. Despite their intimacy, in its aftermath, she couldn't help but wonder what she'd done. Had she indeed taken the first step toward some sort of devastation?

This wasn't her life. And in a blinding bit of panic, she wondered if she had burned some sort of bridge back to her old life. How would it ever be possible for her to return there after — she closed her eyes tightly shut.

It wasn't exactly regret. It was more like being stunned, in a state of shock. The intensity, the emotions that had rolled over her. How could she return to being that quiet, slightly detached, placid soul everyone expected her to be?

*"Be calm,"* she heard his voice whispering to her, even though he wasn't in the room. It was like before, before when she had no

vision. She would hear his voice inside her mind, calling her, comforting her, leading her to places she'd never known before.

*"You should rest,"* he said. *"Everything is all right."*

And a peace but sleepiness settled in. She looked to the balcony door, but he hadn't returned. She leaned over onto the pillow closing her eyes. She would figure it out later, all of it later.

◆

Ethan Garraint quietly pulled on his clothes. Erin was still asleep in the bed. Rather stealthily, he opened the door to the private balcony and stepped outside, leaving the door not completely closed so he would hear if she stirred. The air outside was still slightly chilled, though not intensely, a typical somewhat humid November night in the city. He breathed deeply, trying to clear his mind.

Last night, thinking had not been paramount. He wondered what Brother Guidrade would say — his taking advantage of an innocent young woman, but then again, perhaps he would understand. He had warned him how it would be, and Ethan, or Etienne back then, had not disregarded his words. He had simply overestimated his self-control. He thought he would be able to handle things, to master emotions, to master the wolf within.

He grasped the edges of the wrought iron banister of the balcony. Had he failed? Or was this the way things were meant to unfold? And now, how would they move forward?

He'd learned something of spiritual bonds during his time with the Cathari people. Certain human activities were considered profound initiations to the spirit that lives within, activities such as making love. While modern people assume it is a physical act of no consequence, in truth, it profoundly affects the spirit. It links the individuals together and binds them to each other.

So last night, making love with Erin, his spiritual match, created powerful bonds between them that would change everything.

He closed his eyes, clearing his mind, trying to find the proper course to take now. But also feeling on a profoundly instinctual level that he did not regret anything that he'd done.

He gripped the edge of the wrought-iron balcony tightly, so tightly that his hands ached. He was an old man. At times, he had to remind himself of that fact. He should have accrued more wisdom by now. He should be able to handle this and not have it tear at him like a knife gnashing raggedly at his heart.

She was so like her in ways, both lovely, intuitive, gentle, but strong. Yes, he could feel her stirring beneath the flesh of this Erin Holt, but different. The woman he was touching last night was so compelling to him, drew him like a drug he couldn't resist, but not the same, not as he remembered.

"Reincarnation is not as one thinks. Our spirit clothes itself in a new soul and new flesh every lifetime. So, it is not exactly as though we are living another life, though indeed the spirit is experiencing a new one."

He'd listened to Brother Guidrade, absorbing his lessons but not entirely understanding what he was saying. After all, Etienne, at that point, had been alive for several hundred years already. He would not reincarnate. He would live forever unless, of course, someone managed to kill him. His circumstances were not the same.

"So, what are you saying?"

The old man had smiled with a bit of amusement at him. He knew his pupil's mind had strayed from the matter at hand. "Well, this woman you say you loved so long ago."

"My wife."

41

"Yes, your wife, if her spirit chooses another life, it will be the case with her."

"The case? Oh yes, as you say, a new soul."

"New soul, personality, demeanor, and, of course, the flesh."

"Different body, so what are you saying, it won't be her?"

He had smiled at him then, and he'd forgotten the expression. But there was kindness in his eyes and that ever-present compassion, as though even then, the old man could peer through centuries and sense the torment that Ethan was experiencing now.

"It will be, and yet in some ways, it won't."

He opened his eyes, staring out into a cloudy night sky that had all but muffled out the stars. Why hadn't he taken more time to prepare himself? And how could he begin a new journey now, when he still had so much trouble releasing the old one?

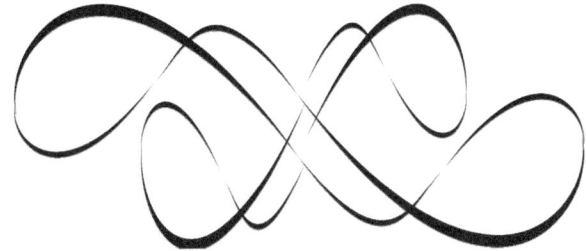

Chapter 7

# ENID

"What is darkness?" she ventured outward.

*"It is the state of one's heart when one rejects the true path."*

She opened her eyes, staring upward into the flickering light amongst the towering trees that sheltered the forest — her forest, as she called it.

She closed her eyes again, reaching out to the whispers in her mind. "What is the true path?" she asked, although it wasn't exactly that she didn't know the answers. It was more that she took comfort in hearing her voice, the Fairy of the Wildwood as she knew her.

*"It is the way of the spirits, child. You must always follow your path."*

"And if I don't, I will fall into darkness?"

She heard the sound of the breeze rise in her ears, and she opened her eyes to see the limbs overhead fluttering in strong reaction to its presence. *"I wish it were that simple."*

She sat up as a chill ran over her. It was that sense, that sense of foreboding that more and more frequently would cascade over her at odd times, shattering her tranquility. "What do you mean?"

There was silence, hesitation, then, finally, the softest of answers. *"Sometimes the path is darkness."*

Again, that drape fell, something, a sense of something coming that frightened her. *"Don't be afraid,"* the voice whispered, attempting to comfort but not being able to thaw that icy fear that had touched her heart.

"I am afraid. I feel—"

*"It is the future."*

"Can I stop it?"

*"I think not."*

"Why? I can avoid whatever it is."

There was silence, and then she felt warmth as though some being lighter than air had wrapped its arms around her. *"Some things are already woven into the cloth."*

"This darkness you speak of."

*"This veil you must journey through."*

She called her the Fairy of the Wildwood, though she knew who she was. It was something that remained unspoken between them. Her mother, her true mother, had died giving birth to her. But when she was only a child of three, she began hearing her singing at night while she was left in the quiet of her room. Then, she began speaking to her when she was not yet ten.

And in her seventeenth year, it began as that future rushed in upon her like a storm, like a cataclysm, one that changed everything for good or ill.

◆

*"Erin."* She heard the whisper, and her eyelids flickered open and closed again. It wasn't him, not Ethan. It was from that other place she'd been dreaming about, the girl in the woods with her long honey-colored hair. And that voice, the one that guided her, the same one she had just heard.

*"Erin,"* again speaking to her now out of that dream. It was an old dream, one she'd had all her life. But not the same dream, just the same girl, always, as though it were some kind of continuing movie, and she would sleep and see snippets of it.

*"Erin, it's time to wake up dearest,"* that voice again. But now it spoke to her with strength.

She opened her eyes and saw the ceiling fan overhead again. The room was filled with light. It must be morning. And then she saw him, sitting in the chair by the French doors that led out onto the balcony. Her heart clutched a bit as the night before came rushing back in vivid depiction. She gripped the covers more tightly as she pulled herself up into a reclining position. After all, he was fully dressed, and she wasn't wearing a stitch of clothing. His eyes took in her movement, but his face was nearly expressionless. "How are you?" he asked softly.

She was nervous. Regardless of the intimacy that had exploded between them last night, this morning, this aftermath felt confusing, awkward, and bewildering. "Um, not sure," she murmured, feeling a chill pass over her in the room. "What time is it?"

"Nine," he answered calmly.

"Wow, really? That late?"

"You were exhausted." She didn't see it but was fairly sure a blush had crept over her.

She nodded, sweeping her hair behind her ears with the hand that was not still clenching the sheets. "Well, I don't usually keep such late hours." His eyes passed over her, and she felt again that crazy attraction to him that had washed over her in a typhoon last night. But what was more than clear in the morning light was that she needed to think, and to do that, she needed to get some distance, just a bit. "I'm really cold. I think I need to get dressed." Something passed over his features, just a glimmer of perhaps a smile, but then it was gone.

"Do you like coffee?"

Strange question, but she decided to go with it. "Yes."

"Well, then why don't I get us some coffee and croissants for breakfast while you get dressed, then we can talk about things."

She smiled and nodded, grateful that he was being so sensitive in what now felt like a bit of an outrageous situation. "Okay, sounds good."

He stood up and walked over to the bed suddenly taking her hand. He felt warm and comforting, but she was still finding difficulty breathing. "Erin, don't worry. Everything is all right."

She looked away from his gaze, just so she could try to put two thoughts together. "I'm sorry, but last night. Well, that isn't the way I usually live my life."

He squeezed her hand, and she looked again into his blue-grey eyes. They looked so understanding, so caring. "Yes, well sometimes changes come upon us so quickly that it takes a moment to assess who we've become in the aftermath."

She sighed, "I—"

But then he'd already bent down to softly kiss her on the lips, reminding her ever so gently how powerful his hold on her now was.

♦

Everything was different in the bright, nearly scorching light of this New Orleans' November day. Ethan slowly walked down Chartres Street to a pastry shop on the corner of Decatur and Conti. He was taking his time, giving her a little while to collect herself and perhaps giving himself time to strategize. It was a skill he had cultivated during the last several centuries of his existence. It sometimes came in handy to plan and consider the possibilities, pitfalls, and consequences of every possible action. But then again, considering consequences after one's actions — and might he add one's impulsive and, in some ways, unforeseen actions — was somewhat a waste of time.

He continued to walk, trying to remember to be aware of his surroundings even in his wildly preoccupied state of mind. He should chastise himself soundly. Who was he kidding, "unforeseen" indeed. After what they had been to each other, how could he possibly describe what had happened last night as "unforeseen." It was almost as though he'd learned nothing over the long, protracted span of his existence. How long had it been since he'd known her before, eight hundred, nine hundred years? How long since he was that impetuous, self-centered brute who had stumbled across such loveliness — not just physical loveliness but the kind within that touches your soul and changes you? It was impossible to explain to someone who had never felt that way, never felt such a profound pull and connection to another being.

He stopped and crossed Decatur Street, sitting momentarily on a concrete bench. He bent his head in weariness. Now, but now, what was right to do? He closed his eyes to think, but all he could do was smell the earth, the foliage around him, as he rode through a forest so long ago.

◆

He did not believe in magic. He was a fighter, a defender, and a knight for the King and Queen. Many of his comrades held such beliefs that mystical beings enchanted or cursed the lives of those who crossed their paths. But he did not entertain such notions. Unless he saw it face to face, interacted, and perhaps battled with such forces, as far as he was concerned, they did not exist. At least in his world, they did not.

He continued to ride onward through the thick forest. It lay some way past the palace of Caerlleon and across the ford of the Usk. He was weary but had been told of the town beyond where he had tracked a disreputable knight who had offended the Queen.

He rode on, feeling a thickening of the air the more deeply he traveled within the wood. Perhaps it had been a mistake coming this way. Perhaps he should have taken the periphery instead, round the edge of the forest. But he was in a hurry, intent on tracking his prey. And he was a man who lived solely in the moment, confident in his skill, his strength, and, at times, animal cunning that gave him the edge in almost every encounter — those of confrontation and those of diplomacy.

Overhead, he heard a brushing and rattling sound, no doubt birds or small animals scurrying at his approach. And then the smell of water. His horse, Uasail, was panting. It would be good to refresh him before he continued onward.

As he pushed on through the thick brush, something caught his eye, a quick movement. He dismounted his white stallion and led him by the reins forward. And then he stopped at a flash of color. It was a figure he could make out sitting on the edge of the stream. There was no doubt that she'd seen him, looking surprised and frightened. But Geraint could not even take that in. He was entranced, completely entranced, and he wondered at that very moment if he should rethink his stance on enchantments.

♦

Ethan opened his eyes, trying to breathe in the present. For it was the present that he needed to deal with now. He wondered if the best thing he could do for Erin was to simply walk out of her life. But as he rose and continued to walk along the hot New Orleans pavement, he knew he wouldn't. Even now, that magic between them was weaving its way into his soul all over again.

# Chapter 8

# FORWARD

E rin waited, wondering what to do — what in the world to do. She couldn't think. Her mind wasn't working properly. Standing outside on the balcony for a few moments, she desperately tried to soak in some calmness, some sanity. But, of course, this wasn't all that unusual. People hooked up this way all the time, all over the world.

But she wasn't like everyone else. That particular fact had been drilled into her soul at a very young age. And this, this didn't feel like anything casual. Strangers weren't usually so intensely tied to one's psyche, not like this.

Memories were flooding back to her now in torrents, conversations, feelings, sharing thoughts — hearing his voice in her mind so often like a comfort. Back then, at times, it was the only thing that had made her life bearable. All those precious moments, it was as though they'd been put away in a box somewhere, buried, until now.

It made no sense. How could she have forgotten him? How could she be missing such a piece of her life for so long? And how could she have thought that nothing was missing and that everything made sense?

But now everything was different, and she did remember.

Who was she? Surely, she wasn't who she thought she was before all of this, the revelations of their connection, and then the intimacy of last night.

She breathed in painfully. The truth was, and she had to be truthful, she wasn't mourning the loss of who she'd been only a day before stepping onto that plane at the Fayetteville airport. It had been growing within her for months, possibly a year — the restlessness mounting. She struggled against a feeling of confinement, as though somehow along the way she'd been shoved into the idea of someone else's mold, a mold forged of expectations and pressures from a world she'd walked into once she'd gained her sight.

And now?

She sat quietly on the edge of the queen-sized bed, waiting and feeling the tears of confusion slipping down her face. It was too much to assimilate, as though the world she thought she knew so well had bent back and warped into something she didn't recognize. It was frightening and drew her in an undeniable and intoxicating way at the same time.

Erin closed her eyes, trying desperately to feel again the way she used to, long ago. The colors floated beneath her eyelids as she tried to reconnect with the life in darkness she used to navigate so well.

♦

Whispers, *"Calm, dearest one."*

"How?"

*"Things shift and change, and we must flow into the change, not try to obstruct it."* The voice was familiar. She should have recognized it but could not.

"I don't know if I want things to change."

She allowed herself to sink deeper. *"Just,"* that soft voice whispered, *"Be,"* barely audible now. Around her, she could smell the earth and then the water so close. And she could feel his hands on her, sweeping her into that spell that was so frightening but that she yearned for.

"Be with me," his voice was husky and impossibly strong.

"I can't," she spoke, but it wasn't the same, not at all.

"Your father has promised you to me already."

She breathed deeply, knowing there was no point in fighting it, although she could already see the darkness approaching them.

"How can I stop this?" She asked the comforting Fairy of the Wildwood.

*"Some things can't be stopped."*

"I'm afraid," she whispered.

"But I will always protect you," he answered. "I promise."

The light knock at the door pulled her back. She opened her eyes, unsure of where she was for a moment. The pull to that other place had been so strong.

◆

Ethan waited at the hotel room door for a moment, unsure if Erin would even open it, but after some moments, she did. She was dressed in a longish off-white tunic and matching pants. Very fetching, he thought to himself. But then again, not as fetching as she'd been last night. But he brushed those thoughts aside.

Her eyes seemed unusually wide and tentative — not frightened. He sincerely hoped, not frightened.

Deliberately, he reigned in his emotions, emotions which did seem hell-bent on getting out of control around this woman. But this morning she needed calm, so he would do his best to show her that she could relax around him.

"How are you feeling?" he asked, closing the door behind him.

"Oh, a little tired," then she glanced away awkwardly. This was going to prove trickier than he'd anticipated, but how, how to get on a comfortable footing.

"Would you like to eat out on the balcony?" he asked smoothly.

She nodded distractedly, "Yes, maybe so."

And then he silently opened the French doors. Ethan wondered how it would be best to proceed here. The emotions he was picking up from her were turbulent and confused. He followed her outside. She wasn't sitting, just standing, gazing silently off the balcony that overlooked the swimming pool in the courtyard down below. Fortunately for him, it was unoccupied because privacy was important now. He placed the bag with the croissants and the cardboard container with the two cups of coffee on the table, then took both her arms with his hands, gently turning her to face him. "Erin, it's all right."

Her face reflected the tinges of surprise at the bold gesture on his part. And then she stepped back, pulling his hands off her in the process. "You have to stop doing that," she whispered.

"Doing what?" he said, not being able to stop himself from smiling. For not the first time, he wondered if the best way to settle all this awkwardness and angst was to take her to bed again. It was not the most politically correct or well-evolved solution, but in the old days, it might have been his first choice.

"Touching me, I-I can't think clearly when you do that. Everything gets crazy and confused."

He brushed her cheek lightly with his fingertips. "Maybe it's better not to think so much."

Her eyes hardened a bit, and he remembered, at least in that other time, she did have quite the temper, seeming calm and accommodating on the surface. But then, once you touched that core of fire — not unlike a dragon being roused from its sleep, well, nothing was the same. "You are a stranger to me and last night I— we—" she stammered.

"Made love passionately?" A quick blush crept up around her lovely cheekbones. She was still so innocent, and how that beckoned him. "And that is not correct. We are not strangers."

She shook her head, "I still don't understand that. How can I not know you and then suddenly remember you?"

He pulled out one of the wrought iron chairs at the table and sat down abruptly. "Wouldn't you like to eat before we get into any of this?"

She crossed her arms in front of her protectively. "I would like an answer to my question."

He pulled the coffee cups from the container, painfully aware that he was stalling. As Brother Guidrade had always said, all things are connected. And in this case, one truth will lead to another and then to truths that no one should have to face after the night they'd spent together. "There simply isn't an easy answer to that."

She pulled out the chair across from him sitting down. "But there is one."

"Yes, of course, but eat first."

Her lovely, wide, greenish eyes were on him, trying to puzzle things out. He could feel it, intently. But the question remained how much — how much was he willing to tell her?

◆

### *1544 Montségur – in the Languedoc region of Southern France*

"It has to do with energy vibration. Everyone emits it — energy. It comes from being alive. And, of course, the vibrational level has to do with how evolved you are, how connected you are to your spirit."

He had to admit readily, at that point in his existence, that he didn't particularly consider himself an intellectual, a pursuer of knowledge, much less wisdom in any respect. So, the words of a very learned and the physically older Brother Guidrade didn't readily penetrate his rather thick skull. "Well, honestly, vibrational energies and evolved souls, I can't see how that would have much impact on the real world."

"The real world you say, my Brother, where exactly do you think we are living? Impact? This is the world, Etienne. Open your eyes. Really open your eyes, and you will see things that are undreamed of."

He began to speak, and then he hesitated, remembering that little nagging fact that he so often liked to ignore — the wolf. There was, after all, a difference between being indifferent and being a fool. And Etienne was no fool. "I understand," he murmured. His companion smiled ever so slightly to indicate triumph but not to rub it in too much. "So, what is the impact of this, those who resonate a higher energy vibration? I imagine it takes much study to achieve such an elevated state."

"Sometimes, but then some seem to simply come to it naturally. Spirit evolution in past lives is cumulative. It's not something that you lose."

Etienne leaned against the balustrade of the fortress at Montségur, considering what he was being told. The concept of living more than one life seemed very far removed from his existence, given how extended his chronological age was already. "How would such a thing manifest, I mean, in a person?"

"Well, extraordinary gifts, perceptive powers, some even can breach dimensions, cross time flows."

"Time flows? What is that?"

"Oh yes, the bends in time, you know that all time is one. We're just given this construct of chronology to facilitate our learning here on earth. Once we don't need it anymore, it will disappear."

Etienne smiled at Brother Guidrade, not wanting to strongly entertain what he was being told. "Have you ever met one of these? I mean individuals able to breach dimensions and time."

The old man looked off into the distance, his gaze settling on the most distant rises of the Pyrenees. "Yes, as have you, Etienne."

"Me?" he said with puzzlement.

"Yes, did you never take the time to note how extraordinarily gifted your wife was?"

A heaviness seemed to drape over them at the mention of her, of Enid. "I believed she was enchanted and, to my shame, a sorceress at one point. I'm afraid I was not a very enlightened man, even less so than I am now."

"It's all right. We're all given the chance to redeem ourselves and learn in the process. Magic? Indeed, some view these abilities as just that. Sorcery? Well, that does take on a different connotation. But yes, your wife was extraordinary, make no mistake."

◆

56

"It wasn't my intent to make you unhappy."

She looked into his eyes. He was staring intently at her in a way that felt disturbing and extremely intimate at the same time. She didn't understand what was happening, what had happened, how she could be feeling this way about someone she virtually knew nothing about. "It's not exactly unhappy." She murmured, sipping the hot café au lait he'd bought her. She glanced away, staring down at the courtyard below.

"So," he said softly, placing his hand over her other one, which was still lying on the wrought iron table. "I should have dropped you off last night and arrived with breakfast this morning. And taken more time courting you?"

She sighed, glancing back at him, feeling that electric thing again, the one that happened when he touched her skin. "Maybe it would have made things simpler."

"And I shouldn't have reminded you about our past connection, the long conversations we would have when—"

"When I was blind," she offered.

He frowned a bit, but it didn't feel like a frown. There was something so elementally charming about this tall, blond, bearded man. The way he talked, the way he put together words, the way he moved fluidly, the smoothness and charisma simply inherent in him that, frankly, she'd never run across in another person. "I suppose you would have preferred to leave all of that forgotten."

She took a quick breath. Is that really what she wanted, to have things proceed down a more normal course? Frankly, she had no idea. "I'm not saying that. I'm saying yesterday I felt like a certain person, and this morning I awoke with the distinct feeling I didn't have a clue who I was."

"And I accomplished this?"

"I don't know, maybe. Yes, most of it, maybe."

He laced his fingers between hers, sending electricity through her skin. "Erin Holt, would you like to take a ride through the city?"

She looked at him with curiosity, so drawn, just drowning in all of this. "I don't know," she whispered.

"I think you need to clear your mind a bit. How about we go get my car, and I'll show you some of the sights."

Again, but with so much less resistance, "I don't know."

"A little trust," he said softly.

And she nodded, ostensibly having nowhere to go but forward.

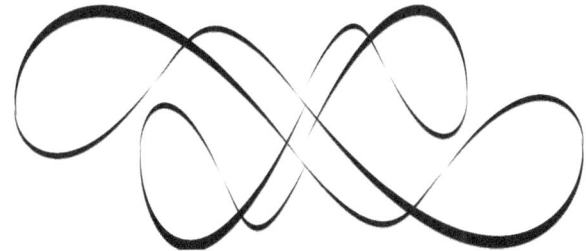

# Chapter 9

# OBSESSION

O bsession

    *It is certainly hard to explain in the present that feeling that had taken hold of me so long ago. Undeniably, I am now a different sort of fellow. Time and experience, and yes, I would have to say, a vast amount of learning has changed or, rather, one might say, has evolved me. For good or ill, that aspect could indeed be debated. Things now are so much more complicated when one can anticipate the layers of effect their behavior can produce on others, on the world about you, and be even able to anticipate far-reaching consequences. Although rather delightfully, I've learned that no one, not even those who like to term themselves the immortal class, could predict all the ripples, all the what-ifs. That is the universe's card that it holds quite close to the vest. Everyone, even me, can be caught off-guard. Of course, on the whole, I could argue quite effectively that my behavior in the last twenty-four hours reflects absolutely none of these higher aspirations of awareness.*

    *But then, back then, things were undeniably simpler. The times I was born in had more to do with survival rather than higher think-*

*ing. Consequently, my thought process operated on a level plateau, ostensibly living another day with some modicum of an honorable code and, yes, gaining as much pleasure from the world as was attainable.*

*And Enid was one of those pleasures, unquestionably. But a pleasure unable to be replaced by any other. She was unique, uniquely fashioned for me — I used to think indulgently when I did think. The man I was, Geraint, was more of a reactionary, quite adept in the moment, with shockingly sharp instincts, but not exactly what might be termed a strategist.*

*Simply put, I saw, and I wanted.*

*It was overwhelming at the onset, and I had to admit, I resented that at first. I was a man in control of his destiny until, of course, I met a woman I could not live without. I begrudged her that power over me. So, I desired to conquer, to force her to yield to me as I within had already yielded to her.*

*In retrospect, I often wonder if ours would qualify as a dysfunctional relationship. I — determined to gain mastery, and she — in her way, fluidly and beguilingly set that I would not. I wasn't even sure that any of it was conscious. And, of course, there was the other matter.*

◆

"She's unique, my daughter."

A little surprisingly, the old man looked truly concerned. He called him an old man, but, in truth, he had no idea how many years he'd lived. His hair was graying, and he carried himself as though he was aged. But in his experience, Geraint understood that time held its sway over people in all sorts of varied ways. "With the utmost respect, I am more than sure there is no other for me. It must be your daughter, Enid."

The elderly man nodded hesitantly, though Geraint could still read trepidation in his eyes. Geraint had competed in the local tournament of the Sparrow-Hawk and brought honor back to the man's family. Asking for his daughter's hand, a knight such as himself who would inherit lands from his father seemed as though that would only add prestige to Enid's family. And it was not as if he expected much of any dowry from the arrangement. Geraint was more than aware that this household had been living in near destitution. "I can see you are fixed on this," was his answer. Not encouragement or appreciation or any sort of response that Geraint might consider predictable. There was no doubt the old fool was beginning to prickle him a bit.

"Perhaps if you were more specific with your concerns."

Enid's father again was silent, then sank into a wooden chair near the long dining table where he had cornered him early this morning. Geraint was a man who did not have much patience. Once he had settled things in his mind, he wanted them settled everywhere else as well. He wanted to wed Enid this afternoon and, in the morning, set out back to court. "My wife, not Deidre, but Enid's mother was an unusual woman."

He grimaced, having no conceivable idea where this was going. "Unusual?" He echoed.

"Indeed, do you believe in necromancers, Sir Geraint?"

"Necromancers?" he replied with some confusion.

"Yes, my boy, necromancers, fairies, otherworldly spirits — the world of incantations, spells, mystics."

He sat down next to Robbert Kinglon. "I will admit I have heard of such beings. My King claims a close connection to what he terms a wizard, if you will, but with my own eyes I cannot confirm their validity."

"Yes," he voiced nervously. "I was once such a man as you. There must be proof, must be something I could feel or taste. I must see firsthand to believe in anything. That was until Enid's mother, Aneira."

Enid's father paused, and for a moment, Geraint thought that perhaps he was finished. But then he continued, his voice low but almost trembling as though it was with great effort that he imparted this information. "Aneira lived in a nearby village with her parents. I met her at a time when I was very prosperous. From the first moment I saw her, I knew, well, I felt toward her as you do toward our Enid. We married within a month of our first meeting. But then her parents told me of something after the marriage. They told me that Aneira wasn't their blood child. That they were given her by a young woman who simply appeared in their village one day. She was with child, was taken in by the nuns of St. Cadoc's Church, gave birth, then disappeared. Aneira's parents had no children, so they raised her as their own. They knew nothing of her origin. Had they known, they told me, well, maybe things would have been different."

"I don't understand. What are you trying to say?"

"Enid's mother was an enchantress, a mystic. She communed with spirits from the netherworld. She was a seer. She died in childbed when Enid was born but has continued to communicate with the girl. Can't you see my boy? They are the same."

◆

Awakening in the darkness of their bedchamber, just the light from the parted tapestry on the window across the room illuminated the shadows, enough that he could see his wife standing next to it, enveloped in the darkness.

A draft drifted across his bare shoulders as he sat up. For a moment, he wasn't even sure it was she, but then the shadow near the window moved, and her form in the long white nightgown became discernible. "Wife, come back to bed," he said softly.

Like a spirit manifested, she turned silently toward him, her long honey-colored hair flying about in the suddenness of her movement. "I did not mean to wake you."

Holding out his hand, "Come back to bed."

They hadn't been back at his father's house more than a month, and yet it still felt to him like yesterday that he had wed his Enid. The time felt so short to him, and the newness of having such an intriguing wife had not worn off. "I could not rest. I was plagued with dreams."

He frowned. It was true there was something unusual about his young wife, so different, an aspect that he did not like to encourage — fancifulness, nothing more. "They are just dreams Enid, nothing worth consideration."

There was silence in the room, and a chill passed between them. "I do not believe that my husband."

It did bother him that his young wife did not seem to hesitate in contradicting him. "I see."

"I have always had visions. I have never deceived you, Geraint."

"What have you seen, Enid?"

"You will return to the King's court soon."

Anger rose in his throat, but he quelled it. He needed to be patient with her. These inclinations would pass. "That is not so. I am needed here."

"The knights blame me for your absence."

"That is absurdity." Now, there was steel in his voice.

"I have seen it."

"In your dreams?"

"No," she whispered. "The dreams are different."

"What do you dream?"

"Disaster," she said with no inflection.

♦

Ethan's hands tingled on the wheel of his car with something akin to anticipation as he drove through the city. Last night, he'd had enough forethought to park his car in a lot that would accommodate it overnight. That the charge was quite hefty didn't faze him. When he did so, he had no idea he'd spend the night with Erin Holt. That possibility hadn't even entered his mind. He'd been acting, reacting, on instinct, very unlike the man he'd thought he'd become and more akin to the one he'd been long ago — the first time they'd met. Well, as they say, old habits die hard.

"Where are we going?" she asked beside him in the car. He breathed in deeply, trying to calm his nerves. He needed to think, think clearly about exactly what he was doing. The woman beside him was confused, frightened to a degree, but that didn't mean for a moment she wasn't as caught up in this connection between them as he was. "I thought you'd like to see some of the city if that's all right."

There was a hesitation, "Yes, I would."

"Just relax, Erin," he said softly, touching her hand and remembering.

*"I scarcely know you, and you want me as your wife."*

He remembered her then. A bit different, the word he might use was fiercer, more determined. *"I believe you want the same thing, my Lady."*

*"How can you know what it is I want?"* she said with determination.

*"Some things are destined to be."*

◆

It was filled with striking and unique variations. That was what impressed her as they traveled through the streets of New Orleans. The French Quarter, even in daylight, felt remarkably packed with divergent influences, historic, yes, but uncomfortable in some respects. Her eyes traveled across the largely European architecture, and she felt, felt much.

"What is it?" He asked beside her, squeezing her hand as they slowly navigated the narrow streets.

"I don't know. This feels—" she laughed a bit, grasping for the words. "Intense is all I can come up with."

"Well, it is very old, filled with many layers of concentrated living."

She drew in a breath, considering. "Concentrated living? You said that before. What does it mean?"

"It means frankly that too much has happened, too often, in a very small space — life, events, leave their mark."

Her eyes continued to boldly take in the sights around her. There were so many people here, different types, traveling these streets. "You mean energy," she whispered. Why did she use that word? Oh yes, it was him from the past. He'd talked of energy in those early days when she had no sight.

"Yes, energy imprints, does it bother you?"

"I'm not sure. It unsettles me. I suppose where I came from was, in most ways, much quieter."

"And do you prefer life that way, Erin? Quieter?"

She felt his hand unclasp hers and his fingertips lightly brush her cheek. The sensation was undeniable. Those sparks that his skin touching hers just seemed to ignite. "I don't know, just trying to adjust a bit."

Once they left the quarter, she began to relax as he headed up St. Charles Avenue. Her eyes grew heavier as they continued to drive. The lack of sleep from the night before had undeniably caught up with her. "It's all right if you want to rest a bit," he said softly.

She leaned back in the seat. "I'm sorry. I'm just suddenly feeling so tired."

"It's all right," he coaxed, his voice gentle yet compelling as she felt herself slip into a light sleep.

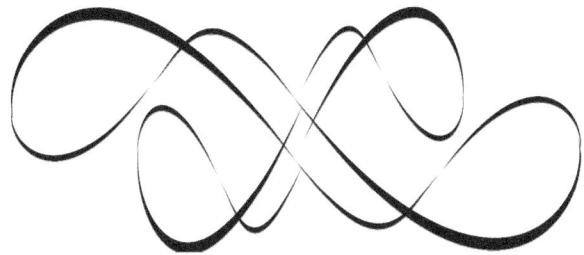

# Chapter 10

# EXPECTATIONS

She moved through his father's castle at Carnant. It was rustic, not nearly as ornate as the King's abode at the Caerlleon Court, but it felt familiar, somehow as though she had or would spend much time here. She walked through the rooms soundlessly, allowing the feelings to overtake her.

Geraint was out supervising and seeing to the needs of the farmers and laborers who worked these lands. His father, Erbin, was in ill health, and her husband would become the Master here upon his passing. There was so much responsibility. That was one of the reasons why returning to court seemed unrealistic at present, although she felt they would before very long as she felt many other things. The halls here were empty, largely deserted, yet to her, they were filled. She could see them, moving about, so many from other times, beautiful women, brave gallant men, a dynasty of life. Then she stopped in one long echoing hallway and turned.

Erin keenly felt the shift in her dream, the separation between them, the Lady with the dark blond hair and herself. They had been one, and yet they were not.

The girl slowly turned around to her, and she now felt herself in that long, expansive corridor as well, standing steadily. The blond woman gazed at her curiously as though studying and trying to make sense of what she was seeing. "What do you seek?" she whispered to her mind, more thought than actual speech.

"Understanding," was the answer she gave.

She smiled strangely, almost as though she pitied her. "Understanding of him?"

"I suppose," she replied.

"Are you sure?" she asked. "These were some of my happiest moments when we were first together, and everything was innocent."

"I need—" and then she stopped. What exactly did she need?

The girl or woman, she did seem very young to her. She looked back at her with those wide brown eyes, staring at her intensely. She didn't know if she thought her beautiful, but she could understand why some might. "Yes, I see that you do. People where you are don't seem to be able to accept innocent happiness. It must be accompanied by knowledge. How sad for you. Understanding rarely brings happiness."

It felt jarring, something in her chest, as though the breath had been somehow pulled from her. "Don't fear it so. It is only some advice," she said softly. "Sweep aside your expectations. They will not serve you well."

◆

Erin's eyes opened abruptly. The car had stopped. She straightened up in the seat. They were somewhere she didn't recognize,

68

parked in the driveway of a single-story pale blue stucco and brick house. "Where are we?" she asked with disorientation. The dream was still with her, so close she felt perhaps she could easily slide right back into it.

"This is my home," he said quietly. "I thought you might like to see it."

♦

It was dizzying. There was light, light flooding in through a huge picture window into the den. And it bothered her, not the light, but something else. The house wasn't very far from the lake, but he hadn't told her that. It was something she remembered from before, from the flood of memories that had rushed upon her last night like a deluge.

He touched her arm, "Can I get you something?"

Erin shook her head, still confused, though amazingly aware of the electrical thing that happened whenever he made contact with her skin. "I don't understand." It seemed to come out in almost a whisper. "I've been here before. I know it now, but that's not possible."

He sat down slowly on the couch behind them. "I think you're pushing yourself too hard. It might be best to let things be for now. The pieces will come together in time."

She turned, looking at him and frowning a bit. "You know, all this partial information isn't sitting well with me. It would be easier to accept all of this if you were just a stranger, someone I'd just met. And we had just begun something new."

He answered thoughtfully, "I suppose I could see how that might seem simpler, but I didn't feel it was fair to keep our past, our connection, a secret from you."

She crossed her arms in front of her. "Not fair? Right now, none of this feels fair, Ethan." How strange it felt to use that name. Geraint, like the woman used in the dream, was the name she wanted to use.

"How can I make this easier, Erin?"

"I-I wish I could say. But I feel pressure to understand, almost as though time is running out."

He continued to gaze at her thoughtfully as though he was considering. But she still felt there was so much, so damn much he wasn't telling her, of that she was certain. "Yes, I know," was his answer.

"So, how about you explain it to me, all of it."

"You're going back to your life at the end of the week," he said flatly.

"Am I?" That was an honest question because even if she got back on that plane to Arkansas, even if she stepped back into that town where she'd grown up, walked back into that protective cocoon her family had constructed for her, she most definitively was not going back to her old life. Too much had changed. She had changed.

Then he stood up, walking toward her, taking her hands in his firmly, and things began to spin, her head, her vision. What was this? What in the world could be happening? "Perhaps, just concentrate on the present," he murmured, pulling her closer to him.

"I need to understand things," she said softly. But it didn't matter because he was holding her in his embrace again, warm, intoxicating, dizzying.

"Yes," he whispered into her hair, kissing her skin, her neck where it was exposed. Again, softly "yes." But then he had scooped her up into his arms, kissing her mouth and taking her somewhere else.

He didn't like feeling this way, didn't like feeling as though everything that mattered to him would be simply ripped away in a short time. It wasn't fair to her, fair to enmesh her in a life that should be no part of her world. But the truth was, he couldn't help himself. Like a man overwhelmed with hunger, who had been denied food, he couldn't help himself, and the truth was that he didn't really try.

"I don't understand what's happening," she murmured. But then he covered her mouth with his. He'd carried her into his bedroom, the bed with the great walnut headboard he had constructed with his own hands. He remembered the energy that had flowed from the wood as he shaped it into a creation of his imagining. But that was nothing like what he was feeling, the energy flowing into his hands as he ran his palms along Erin's skin. It was mesmerizing, hypnotic, and he was experiencing a wild thirst for life that had been absent from his existence for so long, so long that he had become numb to it.

She moved in response to his touch, murmuring in surrender to him. Clearly, she was just as unable to stop this flood of sensation as he was. It wasn't fair to her, but somehow, that thought slipped away in the storm.

♦

There was no sleep these days without the dreams accompanying it. Dreams it seemed she'd always had but now more vivid. Sometimes, she was separate from them, as though watching a tableau from a distance, and other times, as now, she was part of them, feeling them, breathing them, as though she was flesh in some other place.

It felt as though it was her skin, but her mind, her thoughts, and most particularly, her emotions felt different. There was not that controlled, measured feeling, the one she'd completely lost track of over the last few days. Here, there was a wildness to her, a natural spirit that seemed more connected to the earth, the

71

water, the air, and the beasts around her. She was oddly in tune with all that, operating with a connectedness she had never felt before.

"Why do you resist me?" He asked her.

She could feel him just behind her, the heat emanating off his skin. It was overpowering being in his presence at times. He put his hand on her shoulder, and that heat, that power, nearly branded her skin right through the thin cloth of her day dress. But it wasn't painful, although she expected it to be. She was drawn to him, mightily, and that gave him sway over her. "I am certain you could have most any woman you want Sir, except perhaps save the Queen. I'm sure you will find someone more suitable for you."

He placed his other hand on her shoulder, barring her from moving further away. "My Lady, I desire no other woman. I want you for my bride, Enid."

"I'm not certain I'm fit to be anyone's bride."

"Your father has suggested such things to me as well," he said softly, slowly spinning her around to face him. They were outside the house where he had intercepted her. She had desired to make herself scarce, hoping, or so she told herself, that he would feel pressed to move on without her.

"I am not like most women," she answered slowly.

He softly touched her chin, lifting it a bit so that their eyes would meet directly. His were that unusual silvery-blue color, so compelling. She could feel many things looking into them, his steely determination, but something else as well, shadows, shadows cascading across his soul from an unknown source. "Perhaps that is what draws me, Enid. Indeed, you are like no one I have ever met." And lightly he touched his lips to hers, lightly at first but then more deeply as he drew her into his arms. There was that heat, that power surging through her, making her feel strong yet so weak to resist simultaneously. She felt his arm around her waist, drawing her forward into the shadows. She knew what he intended, to make it impossible for her to refuse the marriage. She knew and could have stopped him but didn't. She didn't even try.

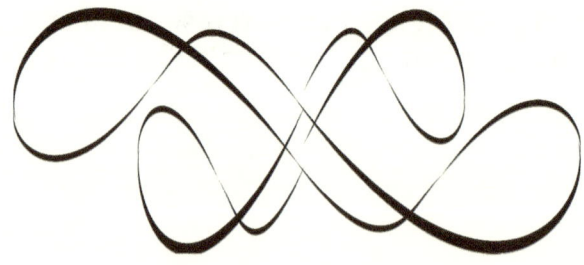

# Chapter 11

# THE WOLF

L ying to Oneself

*Self-deception is a perilous course. Had Brother Guidrade told me that? No, it wasn't him as I remember, thinking back, it was the magician, Houdin, Robert-Houdin, that I'd befriended towards the close of the 1800s in Paris. The man had quite a reputation, reputed by some in later years as the father of modern conjuring. And as I remember, he also had quite the thirst for metaphysical knowledge. We'd made a bargain, back then, an exchange of sorts of mystical items. I provided him with a crystal I'd obtained long ago from a somewhat otherworldly cave hidden deep in the Pyrenees, and Robert gave me a remarkable silver compass he'd pinched from a secret order of monks ensconced near Cordoba in Southern Spain.*

*But I do remember him pontificating during that summer we spent in each other's company so long ago.*

*"Self-deception, my friend, can be calamitous," he'd said. "By all means, deceive everyone else, but not yourself, not yourself. It is*

*more than tragic in the end to be a participant in your own undoing. But being as old as you are, I would think you'd know that."*

*Of course, this was several bottles of wine, and late into the evening when this topic of conversation surfaced. But I've always tried to collect little gems of wisdom wherever they may present themselves, even from the most unlikely sources, which brings me to the present.*

*It seems no more than wishful thinking that I could reconnect with my long-lost love and have it be simple and not wholly intertwined with a bevy of other issues. Yes, I would hope that things could be without incident and Erin and I could simply enjoy our time together. But the threads of life seldom, if ever, allow such disconnection.*

*It was indeed Brother Guidrade who wisely advised me that one choice, one action, always ignites a string of consequences. One movement touches another, touches another, until all the dominoes begin to fall—my words, not his.*

*It was never going to be easy between Enid and me. If I didn't know that long ago, I should know it now. Perhaps there are still many things that I should know.*

◆

Was this madness?

*"Quiet, cold one,"* the whispers wrapped around him securely, binding his skin, his broken bones, the blood that rather than pumping throughout his body, felt chilled within the anticipation of death.

"Who speaks to me?" He gasped from somewhere deep within his soul because there was no speech.

Sharp flashes of memory cut across what was left of his mind. They were attacked by creatures, but not men, demons that pierced the night, four, maybe five.

He could still hear her in the darkness, Enid's terrified screams. "My wife, where is my wife?"

And at that, the whispers tightened around his throat. *"Silence, feral beast,"* it hissed in his ear.

As all faded, he could feel her hands on him, shaking him, hot tears splashing down from her crouched body, her thin, slight form laying across him and sobbing frantically.

Their blood was still sticky on him, and it mingled in her lovely hair that she covered him with. Three he'd broken, and the rest had scampered. But at what cost?

"Please," she sobbed and wailed into the wind, but the chill of death was creeping through his limbs.

*"Do you choose death, accept it, creature of the earth?"* It crooned. What was this that was bargaining with him?

♦

He sat up in the bed. The light of the late morning sun permeated the drapes. His heart was racing in a way that he could not remember it having done for so very long. Beside him, Erin was still asleep, peaceful.

But he was not.

They had spent the balance of the day yesterday, leisurely in the house, catching up on sleep and whiling away the time in each other's arms. The talk of anything outside their current bubble of immediate existence had ceased as they had simply enjoyed each passing moment.

But today was a new day. Moving silently out of the bed, he grabbed his clothing as he left. He walked down the hallway to his study, where he dressed, though leaving his shirt unbuttoned. Sinking into the leather armchair behind the great cypress desk he'd built many years before, he quietly placed his hands atop its cool wood. They still felt as though they were trembling.

The dream was not ordinary. It was not memory, but it was significant. It was prophetic. Something was happening, some unanticipated phenomenon. It felt oddly as though a strange sort of intersection was occurring between what had been and what was happening now. He struggled to collect his thoughts and rampant emotions.

There were things from the past he knew that he remembered from that time long ago. But this, what he'd experienced, this was disturbing and very different.

Ethan closed his eyes and focused, focused on reconnecting with what had been.

"Etienne," the lightest murmur of Brother Guidrade. "Are you certain?"

He gathered and then funneled the powerful energies from within his chakras. "Yes," he said quietly. He must understand.

Almost instantly, he could feel the sun warm his face as he traveled through the forest. *"Leave,"* the spirits within whispered, for they did not want his trespass. That much he could feel intently.

*"Do not breach this space,"* he heard, and even the branches seemed to resist him, but he pushed, traveling onward, deeper, toward the center.

He knew where he was going to that place he'd first found her.

He could even smell the water before he got there. His senses were as they were now, heightened. And she—he could sense her acutely as he came closer. As he parted the wood, he could see her clearly, sitting beside the stream. Her hands rested on the bank and her skirt was hitched up with her legs dangling in the water.

He stopped momentarily, hesitating to disturb her as her eyes were closed. And then she straightened up, turning in his direction, her honey-blond hair flowing around her face. She stared directly at him. "What you seek isn't here," she murmured.

"Ethan," he opened his eyes and looked across the room. Erin was standing in the doorway. She was dressed a bit haphazardly, as several of the buttons of her blouse were still unfastened. "What are you doing?"

He leaned back in the chair, wondering, wondering what, indeed, he was doing.

◆

"Where are we?"

Erin stood on the edge of a precipice overlooking a breathtaking mountain range that stretched as far as her eyes could see.

"It's the Languedoc region of France, near Montsegur."

Ethan turned from her, finding the stone ruins of what had once been a low wall of some sort to lean against. Strangely, he was dressed in black, a black shirt and pants, as he would often be when he visited her so long ago. Those memories, the early ones, had still not become concrete in her mind. They floated about as though disconnected, almost as though belonging to someone else.

In them, she remembered asking why he wore black, and he'd told her that he was a priest once, long ago. But more so that he was in mourning for the people of Montsegur, the Cathars.

"Ethan," she said pointedly, a sudden question occurring to her that seemed more than reasonable to ask. "How old are you?"

His expression was pensive, as though considering how to answer. "You understand that you are dreaming, Erin."

Was she? Just dreaming? Was this real in any sense, past or present? Or was it all tangled up together?

"Why then are we here?" Dream or not, she felt a persistent gnawing inside her to understand.

"I come here often when I'm troubled."

She glanced back again at the breathtaking mountain range in front of them. "You're troubled?" she asked.

"Yes," he murmured. "I have no idea how to move forward."

"Because of me?" she whispered with more instinct than real knowledge.

"You don't understand."

"Then help me. Why is this so complicated?"

"I-" and then he stopped. Erin's eyes moved from him joltingly to a shadow that had appeared beyond him. She waited, catching her breath, then felt herself freeze the moment the beast completely manifested. Quite adeptly, it leaped from behind the wall and landed just in front of Ethan, between them both.

Her breath caught in her throat. In a way, it was mesmerizing, stunning, with its dark gray mottled coat glistening and eyes that burned like blue and silver fire. It was a wolf, no question, but so much larger, twice the size of any she'd ever seen, and different. It moved differently, seeming fully cognizant of both of them and its surroundings. That was the startling thought that crossed her mind. And then it leaned back on its hind legs and bared its fangs to her. "What is this?" she whispered, fear catching in her voice.

"My constant companion," he said quietly and with little emotion. "Don't worry. He won't hurt you. You have his allegiance. Of course, this is only one variation of him. He comes in many, some more human-like, some more beast, sometimes half of each." And then he looked at her speculatively, "I wonder, my Erin, if this is something you could accept."

She sat up in the bed abruptly, the cool draft of the ceiling fan cascading off of her skin. The place beside her was empty. He seemed to have a habit of doing that, just leaving while she was asleep. Her head throbbed from the dream, the terribly vivid dream clinging to her as though she was still standing in the warm, dry air on that mountaintop.

Quickly grabbing her clothing, she was determined to get dressed and find Ethan. She didn't want to be alone. The piercing gaze of the wolf remained with her as though it was still watching her closely.

# Chapter 12

# THE KEY TO EACH OTHER

She stood across the room from him, face pale, greenish-brown eyes wide and unmistakably filled with fear, but fear of what exactly he could not discern at the moment.

"Erin." Ethan stood up. Nearly imperceivably, and, no doubt, only caught by him because he was watching her so closely, she stepped backward a fraction of an inch. Ah, it was clear that she was fearful of him for some reason. Cautiously, he moved around the desk. She held her ground, though, still watching him with those enormous eyes filled with shadows. Once he reached her, he couldn't stop himself from gently placing his hands on her arms. "What's happened?"

She was breathing deeply. He could feel the rhythm in his skin, his blood. Strange how he was so connected to someone whose real flesh-and-blood company he'd actually spent so little time in. But then again, this was a spiritual connection, a fact that Brother Guidrade had so repeatedly drummed into his head. It defied logical sensibilities. It simply was.

And then she closed her eyes, sighing deeply and slumping forward a bit so that her head was resting on his chest in what he could only describe as emotional exhaustion. "It's going to sound ridiculous."

He pulled her closer into his arms, stroking her lovely auburn hair that he'd become so fond of. "Ridiculous things can have their moment," then he added, "Tell me, Erin." However, admittedly, he had that pesky precognitive sense that he already knew.

"It was a dream but a very realistic one," again, a deep sigh that he was not comfortable with. The thought that their entanglement had become so burdensome to her weighed on him considerably.

She pulled her head up and looked into his eyes in a way that startled him, not fearful now, not tired, but seeking deeply. "You were in it."

He let his hands drop. Why, he couldn't say. Perhaps he was a coward. Maybe he'd idyllically hoped they could spend these few days together unencumbered by the truth. "And?" he said because he had no choice.

"There was something with you in the dream, a creature. Well, actually a kind of wolf."

He bravely held her gaze, though now he understood her initial fear. "I see."

"You said it was your constant companion."

And then he smiled. He couldn't help it. What a benign thing for him to say. "Well, what do you think, Erin?"

She looked confused, "What do I think?"

He stepped backward, leaning against the desk but still watching her closely. "Yes, sorry, what do you feel might be a better question."

She crossed her arms in front of her. Though he had an inkling, she had no idea she'd done so. "I-I don't know. It was just a dream. It doesn't mean anything."

He watched her closely, feeling the jagged nuances of what she was wrestling with. Her modern sensibilities told her to ignore what her genuine innate senses were telling her. It was somewhat painful to witness how the mores of a world determined to ignore the old ways ostensibly split its inhabitants apart. "Erin," he spoke softly so as not to further agitate her. "I need you to stop and take a moment. Try to forget what you think you should say, and use your senses, your inner self. And tell me what you truly feel."

Her eyes widened a bit in confusion. He felt the battle within her. When she was younger, when she had no sight, she was not under such scrutiny, such pressure to suppress her very real and tangible gifts. But once she gained her sight, she was forced or perhaps even forced herself to quickly conform to a world that gave no credence to such abilities. Essentially, she had buried part of herself.

"I-I don't know."

He frowned because that was not at all what he felt. She did indeed know but was afraid to say. He reached out and grabbed one of her hands, pulling her closer to him. "It's all right," he murmured. "You know, I was foolish to believe it would take a backseat and remain hidden from you."

Hesitantly, she spoke, "It? What does that mean?"

"Dreams, you know, aren't meaningless. The spirit within us takes flight in dreams, leaves behind our earthly form, and explores other dimensions and realities, revealing truths we cannot easily reach in the physical world."

"Ethan, you're scaring me."

"You don't have to be afraid, Erin. You just have to open your mind to other possibilities." And then he squeezed the hand that he held in his own. "Now, tell me, my dearest one. What do you feel?"

She looked at him almost sadly, and it pierced his heart deeply in a way that he had not thought was still possible. How was it that she could so easily reach him when others were wholly incapable of breaching the ice built up around his emotions through centuries of his protracted existence? "You hold the key to each other, one that is unique and cannot be denied." They were words from the Cathar Master, still so poignant and relevant now.

"I," she stopped herself, so frightened of letting go.

And then he took the other hand in his, perhaps to give her strength, perhaps to provide him with some. "Yes," he said softly.

"It's real," she murmured.

"Yes," he repeated. He wasn't looking at her. He was looking at those lovely, gentle hands he held clasped in his own.

"How can that be?"

And then he looked up into her beautiful eyes that seemed in this moment as though they would engulf him. "Well, it happened long ago when the world was still filled with magic and demons. Although it still is, though much better hidden, one might say."

She shook her head, "I don't understand."

And then he laughed at the twisted sort of perversity of the moment. How did one deliver the news to his lover that he was not a man but a sort of devil? "I am a werewolf, Erin. It's that simple."

And then there was something else in her eyes, a fire that he remembered from long ago and was very glad to see in some respects. Very deliberately, she pulled her hands out of his grasp. At this moment, he realized this would be much more complicated than he had anticipated. "Ethan, that's simply impossible."

◆

She realized, granted not for the first time, how she despised feeling as though she was not in control of things in her life, not in control of her decisions. It was a scar, she supposed, from that huge expanse of time when it felt like everyone else in the world was making decisions for her. That very frustration prompted her to get on that plane from Arkansas and come here alone to New Orleans. And that frustration was now pushing her to wholeheartedly reject this preposterous assertion that the man in front of her had just made.

Werewolf, indeed, did he think she was so naïve to swallow any ridiculous thing he might throw her way? Did he think she was so swept up in this romantic spell, this fog she'd seemed to be operating under, and simply embrace any laughable delusion he decided to feed her?

She didn't stop to think that it indeed had been her dream.

She didn't stop to think that the memories she'd recovered about their relationship before she regained her sight were in her head, her mind.

She was frustrated and, in a rage, born of a life that had left her largely powerless.

He hadn't said anything. He was just looking at her, still casually leaning back against his desk. It reminded her of the first time she'd seen him in the French Quarter, watching her from across the street, with no expression, just waiting, waiting for what she couldn't imagine.

"Aren't you going to say anything?"

"What would you like me to say?" he responded rather flatly.

It felt a bit like a punch. She wasn't at all sure what she'd expected but not this. "You do understand how ridiculous that sounds. Werewolves? They're imaginary, made-up stories."

"Old stories from long ago."

"Yes," she said a little shakily. It felt like she was losing ground, though she didn't know why.

"Where do you think those stories come from? Those old legends?"

"So, I suppose you're going to tell me vampires exist as well."

"I spent a good amount of time with one when I was a priest at Chartres Cathedral in France."

She took a quick breath that felt oddly painful. "What? When?"

He stood up straight but did not walk forward even an inch toward her. "It was around 1350."

"1350? Do you really expect me to believe—" Then she stopped, almost choking on the words.

"Do I expect you to believe me? Evidently not, though I assure you that it is wholly and sadly the truth."

"I-I can't just accept this. I—" And then she felt the room begin to spin, actually quite purposefully spin all around her in a cataclysmic motion.

It made her feel sick. It made her want to drop to her knees, but somehow, somehow, she didn't.

When it finally, thankfully, stopped, she was somewhere else. She was in another room, a cold room made of stone.

♦

"How can this be?"

"Your husband was infected, my Lady. He was attacked by the dark ones, the demons. If he somehow can recover, he won't be the same." The old woman's voice cracked with age. "You must understand. He carries the wolf within him."

Erin was here, in the room, and felt her stomach flip and her knees buckle at what she was hearing. But the old woman, dressed in dark gray robes, was not speaking to her.

The one with the long blond hair, the same girl she had seen before in dreams, was bent over a figure in a small bed, a man, but she lifted her eyes, turning directly to Erin. Tears were streaming down her face. It was so confusing. Clearly, the old woman beside her couldn't see Erin. She just continued to examine the man in the bed as though she was a doctor of some fashion. "He must survive. Whatever is to come, he must survive," the younger woman rasped.

"Then, my Lady, you must pour your life's essence into him, not so much as to deprive you of life, but enough to give him the will to live."

"Anything," she whispered, continuing to stare at Erin. The old crone reached out, grabbed her hand, then abruptly took a knife from her belt and almost ruthlessly sliced the palm. Erin instantly felt the pain cut through her own skin. Without a word, the old woman aggressively placed the bleeding hand across a bloody gash on the unconscious man's chest.

Erin could feel her own palm drip blood and tangibly sense the unconscious man's warm flesh beneath her skin. "You must continue until you feel the wolf stir within him. Only if the wolf lives will the man live as well. They are bound as you are to him."

The room was spinning with dizziness, and Erin was weak, as though her energy was slipping out of her. She could hear moaning coming from the bed and looked closely at the man's face as he turned toward her in his wild thrashing. It was shocking, though she had known it at the start, as she recognized Ethan's face, grizzled, wounded from some great battle, but it was him, nonetheless.

And then the blond woman whispered to her sharply. "Now, you see."

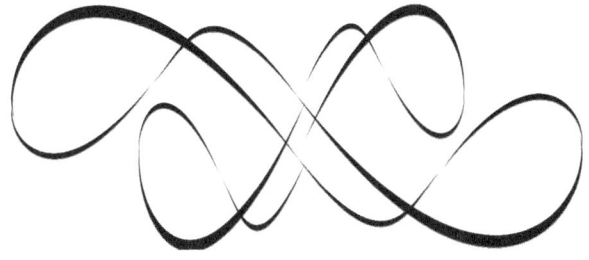

# Chapter 13

# THE SHIFT

It was almost imperceptible, the shift.

Just for an instant, her face changed expression, and her eyes glassed over. And Ethan felt it, although someone else would not have. "Erin," he whispered harshly. And then she blinked, her eyes completely unfocused. She was pale. He took her in his arms, feeling a cool sweat on her body.

Pulling her against him, he could feel her trembling. But she hadn't spoken. Her breathing was erratic. He could sense it acutely through his touch. "Focus, focus on here," he whispered. Because he knew, just as it had been long ago. She was gone. Somehow, she'd pierced the veil between realities.

♦

Her head swam. Where was she? Colors flooded across her eyes in such a painful glaze. Perhaps she was in darkness again, and her sight was gone.

"Erin, focus," she heard in whispers from distant realms.

"You must see clearly and understand what is," another voice, a competing one, pulling her somewhere else.

It was almost like flying, flying through a darkened mist, then careening harshly to the ground. The grass beneath her was moist and high. This she felt as her hands clutched the earth for balance. She whipped her head upwards and could see the luminous night sky and the moon, the full moon peering through the wispy clouds.

She knelt backward, sitting on her legs. There were trees all around, though she'd landed in some sort of small clearing. She struggled to breathe as the chill of the night crept into her lungs. Where was she? What was happening to her?

And then she heard the growl not far from her. It should have startled her, but it didn't. She could feel it reverberate in her chest as though it was part of her. The beast circled from behind the trees, slowly moving with no hurry into the glade. It watched her with those silvery-blue eyes, seeming content to be in her proximity for the moment. She relaxed, quietly waiting. There was nothing else to do.

In seconds, it could overpower her, rip her to pieces, and there would be nothing, less than nothing, she could do to stop it. *"Listen,"* a whisper advised her, *"calm,"* it said.

She drew in a deep breath, trying to relax, then focused on the wolf.

Holding out her hand, she tried to let go of her fear. There was no point. It had her in its clutches if it intended to hurt her. It moved until it stood so close she could feel its warm breath. It had great fangs. She knew this, though it had not bared them. It simply stared with its silvery-blue eyes and gently passed its mouth over her hand. *"You see,"* she could see the blond girl in her mind who had whispered the same thing to her moments before.

The wolf continued to brush her hand, then softly nuzzled her hair. "I see," she murmured.

◆

Ethan had positioned her down in a chair as Erin was completely unresponsive to him. What had he done? What had he brought to this innocent girl's life? How selfish had he been in taking a step toward her, knowing what he was — what havoc that could bring?

She wasn't unconscious. She just continued to stare unseeingly before her. It was like a fugue state. He remembered it from before with Enid.

*"Have you ever met one of these? I mean, individuals able to breach dimensions and time?"*

He remembered Brother Guidrade's words now acutely. *"Did you never take the time to note how extraordinarily gifted your wife was?"*

Initially, when it happened with Enid, he'd discouraged it. It was a conflicted time of great wonders in some regards and great superstition in others. And admittedly, as a younger soul, he sought control over all things, most particularly his wife.

He remembered how her father had ascribed it to some strangeness of her birth. "Enid's mother was an enchantress, a mystic. She communed with spirits from the netherworld. She was a seer. She died when Enid was born but has continued to communicate with the girl. Can't you see my boy? They are the same."

But then again, this was not Enid. Yes, the spirit had reincarnated, but that did not necessarily mean that every characteristic of her former life would carry over into this new one. Nor did it mean that some would not.

He put his hands on the sides of her face, which felt chilled to him. "Erin," he whispered huskily. He tried to focus his energy into her as he'd been taught long ago by the Cathars at Montsegur. He must reach her wherever her spirit had traveled. "Erin, come back," he said anxiously.

And then, suddenly and unexpectedly, he felt an abrupt jolt pass through her body, almost like a spasm. On its heels, she straightened up in the chair and turned to him, eyes now focused on his face. "Ethan," she murmured.

He pulled her aggressively into his arms. "It's all right. Everything's all right."

◆

They weren't talking about it. Ethan had made her some tea and insisted she eat some toast with it that he'd put grape jelly on to give her a bit of strength. It felt odd, the way Ethan was hovering and was clearly so worried.

She read it in his eyes, in his actions, in the concern she felt in his touch, though that he kept masked from his face. It was true. He did care for her.

Had she doubted it?

Yes, the truth was she had. She had little experience with these abrupt "hook-ups," for a better word. Part of her had wondered, despite the connection she remembered between them if maybe this was just a fling for him. A fling, while being exciting and amazing in many respects, would sustain no lasting connection between them.

The truth was that she didn't know, didn't know how he felt about her, and didn't know how she felt until perhaps now. As he sat quietly next to her on the sofa, clearly lost deep in thought, she understood.

It didn't matter how quickly everything seemed. She'd fallen in love with him.

But exactly when she'd fallen was hard to pinpoint as it was a peculiar feeling that just seemed to have always been there.

He reached out and put his hand on her knee. "Feeling any better?" he said softly.

She smiled, "Yes, this helped. I liked the grape jelly."

He nodded, "It came from a local farmer's market."

She murmured, "I'm sorry if I scared you."

And then he grabbed her hand, most possessively, which made her smile. "You did."

"You haven't asked me anything about it."

And then he looked forward as though he was thinking. "I was leaving that up to you."

And suddenly, she felt something, something discordant actually, through his touch. "What is it?" she asked impulsively.

"You're very sensitive." Then he stood up abruptly and walked across the room, standing with his back to her, looking out the den's front window. "I was wondering if you'd like me to take you back to your hotel Erin."

Now, this was unexpected. In fact, it felt like a gut punch. She put the cup of tea on the wooden coffee table in front of her because she was actually afraid she might drop it. "What?" she said a bit incredulously.

He turned around slowly, facing her with what felt like a cold expression. "I've been thinking that all of this has been very unfair to you."

"This? You mean us?"

"I mean bringing my very complicated existence into your life. Do you remember what we were talking about before," he hesitated, "before you had your episode."

"My episode?" she said with uncertainty, still trying to piece together exactly what had occurred. Yes," she said haltingly, "you had just told me you were a werewolf."

He frowned, "I did, and you didn't believe me."

It bothered her, frightened her, really. She didn't like his tone, didn't like the steely way he was dealing with her. "I know. Well, you have to admit it's a bit of a wild card." Then she continued, sensing he was finding no humor in this. "But I do believe you now."

He looked at her strangely, even more strangely than before, almost as though trying to see something she wasn't telling him. "Why?" he said slowly.

Okay, that was a good question. How could she explain? "Well, I-I saw things during my episode, as you called it. I saw the wolf, the one from the dream. And also, something else."

He waited, not moving toward her, just staring intently, "Yes."

Her heart was hammering. This felt so difficult. It would sound ridiculous if she weren't talking to him. "I-I was somewhere else, somewhere I didn't recognize, rustic, not modern, maybe from the past. There were two women there, one old, one young. The young one I'd seen before, in dreams, maybe visions. I'm not sure. She had long blond hair. And there was also a man who was ill in a bed. He had wounds on him as though he'd been attacked. The man I recognized."

She waited for his response, an inclination telling her he understood, but he stood stoically, immobile. "It was you, Ethan, different, but you. The blond woman put her hand on your chest to help you. I think to help you heal. I believe she wanted me to see that."

"Did she?" he said softly.

94

She stood up, though her legs felt wobbly beneath her. "Ethan, what is it?"

"I didn't mean to bring this to you, to complicate your life to this degree. The truth was I didn't mean that you should know me at all."

She walked up to him and lightly placed her fingertips on his face. "Why, then?"

And then he looked at her with such intensity she wasn't sure if she was frightened or compelled, though the truth was probably both. "I couldn't help myself. But if you wish it now, I believe I can make you forget me again."

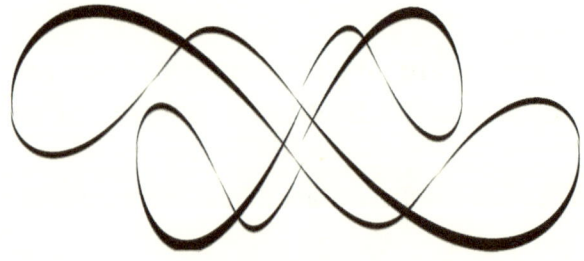

# Chapter 14

# HALLUCINATIONS

"Why do you wait in the shadows?"

There was silence. Of course, she hadn't honestly expected an answer.

"Your eyes will be in an adjusting phase for probably at least another month."

"What does that mean?" she hadn't asked. Her mother had. At that point, Erin was still completely oversaturated with the alien rush of data flooding in from her restored vision, so much light, color, and images, some of which she had trouble connecting with identification.

"What is that?"

And her mother would answer indulgently. "You know, that's your study table that you've used many times, Erin. Here, feel it with your hands," and she did, closing her eyes and running her fingertips across it.

"Oh, I understand." But there were so many things that didn't connect as easily, photographs on the walls she'd never known were there, windows that she'd only come into contact with but rarely. And then, beyond her house, the world was full, bright, with strange things that took some time to merge with her sensation of them when she was without sight.

"I thought you'd be happier," her mother seemed quite perplexed as to why she was not as delighted as the rest of her family.

"It's a lot to process," she would answer. But even she could see that it disturbed them how she was struggling, so she stopped. She stopped letting her feelings out and instead struggled within.

The shadows in her bedroom seemed to fluctuate.

"You'll see flashes of light, maybe even double exposures, and carry over hallucinations for a bit."

"Hallucinations? What does that mean?" Her mother, Marion, had asked.

"It's an unusual phenomenon. It takes a while for the eyes to reorient to their function in the body. They've been out of commission for so long. Sometimes, there is a delayed communication process. Thus, images appear that might be out of time sequence. Just give it a while to settle down, and let us know if it persists. All right, Erin."

She'd smiled and nodded. How would she know if she was hallucinating if she wasn't at all sure what was supposed to be there?

She sat up in bed, focused on the corner of the room, even though it was mostly dark. The only illumination was a nightlight in the hall that slightly crept under the door. She preferred no light, but her mother insisted. "You need to adjust, Erin. Everything is different now."

Once more, she thought she saw fluctuations in the shadows. But then again, perhaps these were those adjustments they spoke of. "So, it's all right if you want to make yourself known. A lot of what I see now is supposed to be nonsense, so I can disregard you if necessary," she said lightly. Why? No idea, except that just about everything was getting to be a bit much now.

She leaned back against her white headboard. For so many years, she had no idea what color it was, just feeling the lovely little shelf built into it where she would stack her favorite braille books. Of course, they were still there, though they had been untouched for this last month. She was now learning the sighted language, at twenty, learning to read again, though granted, it was easier as she already knew the alphabet, and words just had to consciously link between image and what she used to feel with her fingertips. It had been a crazily busy month of catch-up. "So, nothing, huh?" She said whimsically aloud. "Too bad I was in the mood for a distraction."

And then things flickered oddly. Her eyes felt like they shifted, and there was a stab of pain in them. She put her hands up, covering them for a moment. Distracted and, yes, panicky, it crossed her mind that she was losing her sight again.

She'd had dreams, countless ones about waking up in darkness. And honestly always being confused as to how she felt about it. Now, she wondered if it was happening. Should she call out for her parents?

"It's all right," she heard a murmur from the corner of her room, those pesky shadows that seemed to want to spring to life. She took her hands down from her face, even though her eyes felt as though they were stinging.

"I'm sorry. It's energy. I didn't realize you'd be so sensitive to it."

Her vision was still blurry, though beginning to settle down. "Who are you, a hallucination?"

"Maybe," the voice was masculine and more than that familiar. "Just relax," he coaxed.

Should she call out? Was she in danger? A thousand possibilities raced through her mind, but she couldn't find a strong inclination within herself to do much of anything. She could make him out better now, still standing in the shadows talking to her.

"Do I know you?"

"You did, Erin, once, but I think it's fading. I just wanted to make sure you're all right."

What to answer? Then again, that wasn't even a question. Maybe an answer wasn't required. "I don't know," she said without emotion.

"Yes, I can see that. You know the best thing is that you just let go. Let go and see how things unfold. Nothing needs to be perfect, my love. You simply need to move easily, unencumbered from one moment to the next." The voice was so comforting, so familiar, and undeniably felt oddly intimate. He'd said, my love. Outside of her parents, no one had ever said that to her before.

She tried to peer through the darkness but still couldn't see him. He was a form, a person, but deliberately cloaked somehow. "That's not easy," she murmured.

"I know. Just remember. Things can't always be controlled. Sometimes, you simply have to ride events and unclench your hands. Let the sand flow easily through your fingers."

"Sand?"

"Time, events, possibilities — just a metaphor. Let everything breathe."

At that, a wave of sleepiness began to overtake her. And she couldn't help but wonder if she was dreaming. "I'm not sure I understand, but I'll try." And then an odd thought crossed her mind. "I won't remember this, will I?"

"Sleep now, my love." And then she did.

◆

She let her hand drop slowly as she stared into his eyes with a measure of disbelief. Ethan had just told her he could make her forget him. And in the moment it took her to absorb that fact, she realized that she was enraged. "What did you say?" she said in a soft but steely voice.

"I said if you wish it, I could make you forget me."

Then she stepped back deliberately. "Oh, okay, that's what I thought I heard."

Abruptly, she turned on her heel and walked out of the room.

◆

Ethan stared after her, feeling stunned. He'd thought. Well, it's hard to say what he'd thought, except that all of this, the revelations about him, would be too much for her to handle. But then he remembered another face from the past, soft and compliant but iron beneath that pliable surface.

What a stupid man he was at his age. He really had forgotten exactly who he was dealing with.

He followed her into the den, where she was staring out of the picture window that overlooked the back patio. He stood beside her silently, waiting for her to speak because, just being near her, he could feel undeniably calamitous emotions.

"For a while," she began, "I would look at things, like that stone birdbath outside or even the rooftop on the house next door and have no idea what they were. Constantly asking, what is this? What is this? Why is it here? And trying to connect it to the things I knew. Then, all of a sudden, it wasn't as hard. It began to flow so much easier. I didn't know a birdbath, but I'd heard the birds, so this was a place for them. And I hadn't touched a roof, but I lived in a house that needed a covering because of the rain that I knew, that I'd heard, that I'd felt on my face, my hands. At first, it all seemed impossible, and then it wasn't."

She turned to him, with tears streaming down her beautiful face, and he felt a pain in his heart — stupid man who had under-estimated the strength of the woman in front of him. "And you know what, Ethan, not for a moment, did I take the easy way out. I went through it, and eventually, it became easier. I know what you did. I know you made me forget you once before, but if you dare to try that again—"

He smiled. He couldn't stop himself. "Are you threatening me, Erin?" he said softly.

"I am telling you that I won't allow that again. If I decide to leave you, I do so of my own accord, not because you have manip-ulated me."

He reached up and lightly touched the tears on her face. "Manipulated is a strong word, my love."

And then she frowned at him, "I'm angry."

"I understand, but if you live in my world, everything changes."

And then she stared at him in a way that reminded him so much of the other. His Enid from long ago, taking on the horrible realities that had befallen them. "Everything has already changed."

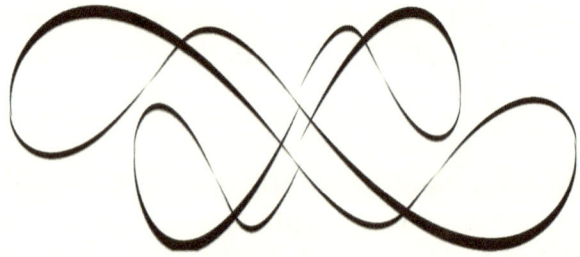

Chapter 15

# POISON

S ometimes, when you open a door, you can't begin to control what rushes in — or what floods inside.

All of it was tabled, any more discussions of what he was, the life he'd led, the fact that he was over half of a Millennium old, and the daunting reality that she, Erin, had just made twenty-six.

It felt natural, however, to be in his arms, to not be inhibited, to let him be her lover and to be his. She had asked him about children because she couldn't help it, given the number of times they'd been together. And he had answered a bit solemnly that given what he was that wasn't a possibility for them.

But even that didn't seem to matter to her now. Within this strange haze they seemed to exist in, she could no longer remember what her dreams of the future had looked like. Had she expected one day to marry, have a family, or perhaps just live her life alone? Or had she always had hidden dreams, fantasies of this blond man rescuing her from what was ordinary and sweeping her into a fantastical existence? Maybe, maybe just like this, because this time with Ethan didn't feel like real life — or at all, what she'd been taught that real life was supposed to be.

It wasn't easy. Her pragmatic side indeed wanted to label, to categorize, not to be so quick to let go.

But what did it mean?

Who were they to each other, and who would they be? All unanswered questions that didn't seem to be getting answered anytime soon. So, instead, all of this remained unaddressed, and on this second day, an extraordinary day, they ate a leisurely lunch that he had picked up from a nearby restaurant while she had slept in his bed.

And, of course, dreamed.

♦

"Enid, what have you done?"

"Nothing," she murmured. But she could feel the change inside the girl — the girl with the long blonde hair. When she found her today, she was sitting outside the cottage where she'd last been with Geraint and the healer. She was sitting alone under a fruit tree.

From where Erin was, wherever that might be, she could see small red apples blooming above her. The girl abruptly glanced up from her prayers because it was clear she'd been praying and looked right at Erin, though she wasn't confident she was really there at all.

"Closer," the golden girl whispered. Even from where she was, she could see her eyes were different. They were not as clear amber as before but somewhat darkened.

There had been a change. The girl was altered, but exactly how was unclear. "Where is he?" Erin asked impulsively within the dream.

Somehow, she, too, moved beneath the fruit tree, sitting across from the girl, the woman. Why did she always think of her as a girl?

"I am younger than you."

"And they call you Enid."

"Yes," she said softly, but she did not smile. Erin could feel even more now — the feelings of the girl, what was happening within her — a battle beneath her skin.

"It's the poison," she muttered with irritation. "When I poured my lifeforce into Geraint, some came into me — the price," she breathed deeply. "It is a fire inside me, anger from the demons." Then she sighed deeply, painfully so that Erin felt it, "but it is no matter. It will help him hold on to his humanity, though it will be a struggle."

"And what about you?" Erin asked.

She smiled grimly. "I suppose I will lose a bit of mine. It is a sacrifice. There is always balance."

And then unexpectedly, though what could be unexpected in a dream, she stretched out her hand. "Unless you'd like to take some of the fire from me," and she laughed softly. "It might be of use to you."

◆

Erin opened her eyes abruptly. She was alone in the bed, but a paper was beside her. On it was written —

*Be back in a little bit. Rest well, Ethan.*

She touched the note lightly and felt his energy drift into her fingertips. She breathed in sharply, then sat up and looked around. Maybe it was her eyes, but she could see it everywhere, colors bouncing off the furniture, reverberating across the room, a spectrum of dancing light. It was dizzying and disorienting.

She put her hands over her eyes.

"Stop it now," she mumbled shakily.

She breathed deeply, trying to calm herself, slowly taking her hands down from her face. It had stopped, thankfully, now just the room again.

Reaching down onto the floor, where she'd left her clothes, she grabbed her shirt and pulled it over her head. It was too much, too much happening so quickly.

First, this affair, or whatever you call it, with a man she didn't know but actually did. Then, it turns out he's a supernatural being, a werewolf no less, and then these bizarre phenomena happening to her, the whole room bleeding a spectrum of pulsating color.

And also, of course, all these strange medieval dreams with that mysterious girl. She felt keenly as though she truly must be losing a grip on reality.

"*Stop, Erin,*" it was a whisper, a strong, comforting one taking hold. "*Try to stop thinking, child, and take hold of only one moment at a time.*"

But it was no good. She was breathing erratically as though she were caught in the midst of an increasing panic.

"*Just focus. Draw a simple breath.*"

It was that voice, the one she knew from long ago.

"*Now close your eyes and relax, rest.*" It was a struggle, but she could feel a soothing energy seeping in. Slowly, she could feel herself begin to float away on a sensation of calmness. "*Good, now sleep for a while, child, and we will help you.*"

♦

He knew he hadn't earned it but felt somewhat easier about things. Erin knew now what he was and seemed to be taking it better than he'd expected. Having learned the truth, it was also more relaxed between them, calmer. Of course, there was much to puzzle out about the future, about her future. But for now, there was peace, and he was old enough to know how rare that could be and how one must treasure it once it appeared.

As Ethan turned down the street leading to his home, he immediately noted an unfamiliar red sportscar parked on the side of the road in front of his house. His heart dropped just a notch as he could keenly sense this particular presence before arriving at the driveway.

"How fleeting is peace," he grimly murmured as he turned in.

Deliberately, he left the two catfish po'boys he'd gotten for their late lunch in the car as he stepped out onto the driveway and waited. Almost immediately, the door of the red sportscar opened, and a tall, slender man with black hair in a dark shirt and pants stepped outside, closing the door behind him. Ethan had distractedly hoped rather than believed that his senses had been wrong. "Keeping a low profile, are you Kian?" he commented dryly.

And then, the man smiled broadly, flashing overly white teeth that Ethen recalled well from long ago. "Well, a little indulgence never hurt anyone, does it?" Then he tacked on with a lilt in his voice, "And I guess you would know all about that."

Ethan steeled himself within because the last thing he wanted to do was spend the brief time he had left with Erin, embroiled with another immortal.

# Chapter 16

# A WARNING

He slammed the car door behind him with the force of his frustration. Who was it that had said trying to control life's events was like opening the door to chaos and welcoming it inside? Oh, that's right. It was that slippery old magician, Houdin. Better to ride the tide and be adaptable was his advice. Well, now seemed possibly the moment to adjust course.

The slim olive-skinned man just stood there unphased, content to remain standing in front of his red sportscar, reflecting little expression. Ethan wondered if they should just draw pistols and be done with it. But then again, that probably wouldn't solve anything unless of course, they were silver bullets. His eyes passed over the brightly colored jaguar. "Having a mid-life crisis, Kian?" he asked in a clipped tone.

"Well, for that to happen, it would follow that one would have to know when your mid-life was occurring," he replied flippantly in that accent Ethan recalled from long ago. It had always reminded him curiously of southern Italy.

"Why are you here?"

And then that brilliant smile returned. "You don't seem too pleased to see me, Brother."

"We were never Brothers."

And then he frowned with a bit of theatrical flair. He'd forgotten how animated this one was. "That's right, the only Brothers you acknowledge are all those poor souls that perished at Montségur. Well, that was always your choice to be a loner, not ours."

"This isn't the best time," he replied more crossly than he'd intended.

"You have company?"

"I do," he said flatly.

Kian crossed his arms before leaning against the red sportscar as though he were settling in for a protracted visit. "Yes, seeing as you're pressed for time, I will get to the point. I was directed to come here to see you by a seer, no less. At least, she used to be a seer, though now she's one of the pack."

"Get to the point, Kian."

"You seem altered, Geraint, more on edge, fiercer than I remember you for some time — almost as though you have something to protect now. It is remarkable when we find something or someone to invest us in this world again after so long."

He frowned, wondering with irritation precisely what it was going to take to get rid of this particular individual. "If you're tired of living, Kian, I'm more than sure someone could be found to put you out of your misery."

"Oh, I wasn't talking about me. I have no problem finding distractions to keep me interested in living. Evidently, just as you've found a distraction, you are anxious to get back to, whoever you might be ensconced with at the moment Geraint."

"I'm going by a different name these days."

"You know, I was never one for disguises like you were. Although I did appreciate Le Guerrier, it had a ferocity to it."

"And you were saying why you were here."

Kian grinned in that eerie fashion that made the hair on the back of Ethan's neck stand on end. It was more than evident this old wolf had an agenda. "Yes, I digress — no time for a friendly catch-up, all business. You haven't changed that much, my friend. In any regard, the seer in question sent me your way. She said you'd be reconnecting with the powerful witch, you remember, the one imbued with our essence."

He felt a distinct tingling of danger animate his nerves. "Enid died long ago, Kian."

"Yes, and she was quite the force, wasn't she? More so, I think, than even you anticipated."

"As I said, a very long time ago."

"Yes, true, but there's someone new now, isn't there? Someone bright and shiny and new, isn't she?"

♦

The early days were madness. That much he remembered. He'd felt more than sure that he would never fully recover his reason again. And Enid, Enid's eyes watched him closely, relentlessly.

Once they'd returned to court, they spent only a short span of time there.

"What's happened to me?" he'd asked her in the darkness of their bedchamber.

"You need to rest, my love. It will take a while to recover. The attack you fended off in the land of Tabriol was fierce. It caused great damage."

"I scarcely remember it," he'd murmured with confusion.

"For a time, I thought you had not survived. Then miraculously, you came back to me."

"I'm not even sure what attacked me. It seemed like men, then not, some sort of aberration."

"You protected me, my love. If you hadn't, they would have killed me."

"Did you see them, Enid," he'd asked through the shadows.

"Yes," she replied quietly.

"What were they?"

She seemed to hesitate at the request.

"Enid," he pressed.

"They were demonic creatures, a blending of wolf and man."

"Are you certain?" he asked with some disbelief.

She was silent for a time, and then he felt her soft hands lightly touch his fevered brow. "Yes, my love, I'm certain."

♦

He led Kian through a gate to a patio at the back of the house. There was a facsimile of a courtyard there with a black wrought iron table and chairs near a small brick-laid fountain. As Kian settled into a chair, it crossed Ethan's mind that he might need to kill this man, and he used that word lightly.

But then, that might not solve the problem. Despite his solitary existence, wolves did tend to congregate in packs. So, making one disappear might just incite more to follow his trail, and that was something he didn't need. What he needed was to get rid of him and find a way to keep Erin apart from all of this.

Kian looked around the patio, seeming unimpressed. "Very low key, my friend, but I suppose that is how you've survived on your own for so long."

"No flashy red Jaguars."

He shrugged, "Pity, drives like a dream."

Ethan leaned back in his chair, wondering if he was obliged at this point to make a deal with the devil. "So, you were saying."

"Oh yes, the seer sensed great power emanating from this city. And then she pinpointed you as its source."

"Me?" he said a bit dubiously. "Well, Kian, sounds like your seer might be a bit off base. My so-called powers aren't much different than your own, nothing noteworthy, really."

He frowned, "Sorry, friend, let me clarify. You are the common denominator around which this power emanates."

"Common denominator? Sounds sketchy, Kian. Maybe you might want to get yourself a new seer."

He frowned, "Stop playing games, Geraint. The woman you're with is linked somehow to the witch from long ago. That much is clear."

Ethan nodded, understanding that the dancing around was over. "All right, Kian, let me be explicit with you and any more of your Clan who might feel the inclination to come lurking in your footsteps. The lady in the house is under my protection. I will not tolerate any of you coming anywhere remotely near her. Do you understand? You know my reputation, Kian. These are not empty threats."

And if it were possible, it seemed that Kian's olive skin had blanched ever so slightly. "Yes, Geraint, all of us are aware of how formidable you can be and have given you a wide berth over these many years as a consequence. But let me just say as a warning, there are all sorts of dangers, seen and unforeseen. Tread with caution."

"Always," he said quietly.

In the next moment, Kian abruptly stood up, "Yes, well, old friend, I will reiterate. Our seer perceived the potential for great danger here, for you, and all around you. I will leave you now to your fate, the fate of your own making—"

"As it has always been," Ethan murmured softly.

◆

*"Enid,"*

She heard them, the whispers from the Fairy of the Wildwood as she walked through the castle in Carnant, but she did not answer. She did not want guidance. They were remote enough here that she'd been able to contain him during the first cycle of the moon. The healer in Tabriol had told her of the transformation that would take place and supplied her with herbs to give Geraint that would hopefully contain him. In that land, they were more than familiar with the creatures that had brought this calamity down upon them.

During the last passing of the moon, she'd been able to keep him confined in one of the palace's keeps, tied to his bed.

The servants were told he was contagiously ill and only his wife would tend to him. She was more than amazed that it had worked. Of course, she was forced to weave several spells that the healer Bethel had taught her. It had been difficult and draining for her, but with these and the herbs, she'd been able to confine the transformation — though she'd exhausted herself in the efforts.

This morning, Geraint was out riding again, attending to business in the province, seemingly recovered. It disturbed her tranquil mind. How could she control him every cycle of the moon? The servants would become suspicious. How could she possibly manage this?

*"Enid,"* the voice swirled around her powerfully. It tried to embrace her, but she pulled away. She didn't need comfort. She needed strength.

*"Enid,"* this time, it came to her so strongly that she jolted in her aimless pacing. *"Enid, you must tell your husband. You can't continue this way alone."*

And then, on its heels, there was another voice, not soothing but hard and abrasive. "Yes, Enid, you must tell your husband, or we will claim him."

The room flickered for an instant before her eyes, making her feel as though she'd fallen into blindness. Then, after a sudden swirl of dizziness, she found she was elsewhere, in a chamber made of dark stone with a massive fire built up in a hearth at its center.

"What sorcery is this?" she muttered frantically.

At that, a figure walked out of a shadowed corner. "This is your sorcery, my Lady. I just made use of some of your untapped power."

The man before her was imposing, frightening her with his long red cloak, bronzed skin, and eyes, so unnatural, nearly pale gray in color. "Who are you?" her voice shook with fear.

"I am Lapetus. Surely you recognize me, Enid. We met you the night we took your husband, Geraint, into our Clan."

"Recognize you—" she stumbled, then the insidious terror crept into her, "the wolves, you attacked him."

"We have tried to call him, claim him many times since that night. But something has prevented this."

She stepped back, shrinking from him, but her back came up against a frighteningly cold wall. "I do not understand."

"Don't be so humble, Lady. We can smell your power, how you drew our life force into yourself to mitigate his indoctrination. So, in some ways, I could call you Sister."

"Just leave us alone. Leave him to me," she tried desperately to sound strong, but every inch of her was trembling.

"To you?" he smiled broadly with almost a grimace. "Is that really what you want? Such a burden for a young wife. You have no idea the hardship you are taking on. Let us ease it. Give him over to us."

She shook her head, muttering emphatically, "No, no, Geraint is mine, my husband."

"Is he truly, Lady? And the wolf within him, do you claim that as well? You can't keep it caged forever."

She straightened up, suddenly feeling an unexpected rage replacing the fear. "Step back, dark creature." And then, with a power of focus she didn't know she possessed, Enid willed herself back to the castle at Carnant. Once the roaring stopped raging in her ears, she fell to her knees in complete exhaustion. And then she tilted her head up, peering forward and reaching her hand outward. And from the midst of the dream, Erin felt the energy ripped from her chest. She sat up in bed trembling and saw Ethan standing in the doorway.

"What happened?" he said in a voice laced with profound concern.

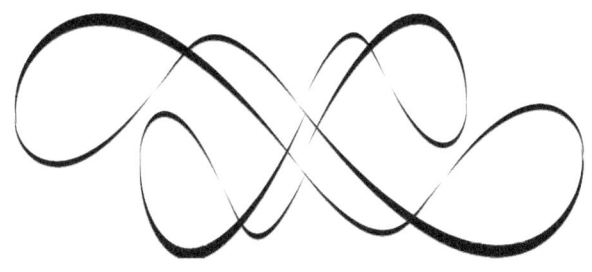

# Chapter 17

# DOWN A GRASSY HILL

**E**rin could see Ethan standing in the doorway, but then her vision began to fade, to blur, and the room spun around her. She felt him grasp her arm but couldn't focus on him clearly. Her sight — panic began to rise in her. Was it her sight, failing again?

"Erin, focus," she heard his voice, like an echo in a distant chamber.

*"No, Enid, this is not the way,"* a whisper in her mind that she had heard before in her dreams.

But things continued to spin uncontrollably, and she felt herself slipping down, almost oddly like rolling down a grassy hill. And then it became tangible. The bumps and sharp twigs bit into her arms, but now she wore long, velvety sleeves.

"Have you lost your wits?" a familiar voice but altered somehow. She pulled her arms more closely inward, though it did nothing to stop the momentum. She'd never done this as a child, never rolled down a hill. From such a young age, she was protected, kept in a cotton-filled box so no harm would come to her.

But this, this was going on forever, spinning downward, down the slope. Was there no stop to it? Would she end up smashed to pieces at the end of things? "Enid, you're being reckless, my love."

That voice, so rich, so filled with vigor.

And then, finally, it did stop, and she sprawled uncontrollably upon the soft, moist ground. She didn't sit up. The breath had literally been knocked out of her. Deliberately, she squinted her eyes shut. This wasn't real. She must still be caught up in a dream.

But then, there were hands on her, solid and decisive hands pulling her up with no hesitation and utmost authority. "You little fool," he whispered huskily, brushing her clothing off as though he had the perfect right to do so. "I didn't expect you to actually take my challenge seriously."

"I take everything seriously," she answered in a vibrant voice, though it was not Erin's answer. It just came forth spontaneously from her mouth.

"Now, open your eyes, wife, and let me make sure you haven't addled yourself to oblivion."

Open her eyes? She dared not. Erin struggled against the compulsion to comply. If she did, would this dream turn into something else?

She focused her mind back to Ethan standing in the bedroom doorway, his eyes filled with genuine concern. With all her determination, she reached out to him, to his arms.

"*No!*" a stringent voice cracked out, this time from somewhere within her. But again, she concentrated intently, battling her way back to her own skin.

♦

Ethan knew the moment he walked into the bedroom that something very disturbing was happening. He could see Erin lying on the bed, tossing back and forth as though caught up in an upsetting dream. But more than he could see, he could feel the energy around her — thick and fluctuating, a very low vibration that manifested almost as a gel surrounding her body for several yards.

It wasn't the first time he'd seen such a thing manifest, but it usually accompanied some dark magic, a self-serving spell.

And then abruptly, she sat up, staring at him with wide, glassy eyes. "What happened?" he muttered with a tinge of panic. But her eyes began to flicker wildly as though something unseen was controlling her. He was by her side in seconds, catching her as she began to faint. "Erin," he murmured, frantically pulling her into his arms. He could feel it when he touched her warm, feverish skin, as though she were covered in that malevolent energy. He pulled her against him, cradling her, trying to focus his own energy into her so that she could fight whatever was attacking.

He leaned her back onto the bed, still holding her. She was murmuring under her breath. Then, he froze in understanding. No, it was chanting, chanting in a very old language — Celtic, he recognized. And suddenly, her eyes flickered open, glazed, and unfamiliar.

A slight smile lit her lips, but it wasn't a smile he recognized as Erin's. He'd never seen such an expression touch her face, nearly triumphant. "Geraint," she whispered with a husky voice.

His breath caught in his throat as he understood. "No, no, Enid."

And then in the next moment, her eyes rolled upward. He could feel a tremor pass through her body, like a spasm.

He began to shake her out of panic, worrying on some level that she might be dying in his arms. And after a second, her eyes flickered open again. This time it was the warm light of the woman he'd spent the last two days with. He pulled her up into his arms tightly, whispering. "It's all right, Erin," filled with a deep dread that his words were not true in the least.

♦

The first thing Erin did was bathe. Even though her head was pounding from the disorientation of the dream and possibly hunger, Ethan had insisted that she shower. Once she finished, she found the white robe on the bed that he'd left for her.

She struggled against the peculiar feeling of being disconnected as though she was inexplicably tethered elsewhere. Truly, it would take so little to drift off again to that other place.

And Ethan, well, he seemed different as well, lost deep in thought, not at all the same man she'd been spending this whirlwind romance with. This new Ethan Garraint was somber, focused, and determined in some inexplicable way.

That peculiar dream with the blond-haired woman, ever since then, everything seemed to have shifted. After her bath, they finally sat down for a very late afternoon lunch. Again, her companion seemed withdrawn, and Erin wondered if she'd done something to upset him.

Once they'd finished and cleared the plates, he unexpectedly took her hand and led her into the den, to the sofa. This time he didn't sit next to her, instead settling in an armchair across from her. "Please tell me what's wrong, Ethan." She said impulsively. The anxiety couldn't be suppressed any longer. The words simply burst out of her.

But it did nothing to lift the gravity of his mood. "Erin, it's all right, but I need you to do something for me. I need you to think carefully and tell me everything you've been seeing and experiencing since we've been together."

"I don't understand," she said hesitantly.

"Please try, particularly the dreams, in detail if you can."

"Dreams? But they don't really mean anything," she answered slowly.

"That's not true," he said gravely. "Sometimes they are the only glimpse we get into what is really happening."

She answered, still feeling a bit bewildered. "Well, I told you about the wolf."

"Yes," he said, "but what about the woman? The woman with the blond hair."

She opened her mouth to ask how he knew about her but then stopped. She had to think, think back to when she first saw her.

♦

There are no coincidences.

He'd run across this truth many, many times during his exceedingly long tenancy on this planet Earth. Perhaps, it took a while for its gravity to seep into his consciousness. After all, he didn't begin his life as much of a thinker, more of a warrior, he liked to believe. But time and experience and more than that, the long years had taught him to view the landscape in a way that most were not given the same opportunity to do so.

Two truths reared their ugly visage in this disrupted present he and Erin Holt occupied. There are no coincidences, and more importantly, the other one. Everything is connected.

His tutelage with the Cathars at Montségur had taught him much about life, about the spirit, and about energy. Once Erin had told him in great detail about the visions, and he did say visions rather than dreams, that she had been experiencing connecting her to Enid, she went to rest. She couldn't understand why she continued to be so tired, but Ethan knew without question that it wasn't just fatigue. Although this day of theirs had been exceptionally active, it was that she'd been deeply drained of energy.

Once she'd gone to lie down, he used a technique he'd learned long ago to put a protection around her so that her spirit would not travel nor be drawn to realms that might place her in further jeopardy. Of course, this wouldn't last. She was a powerful spirit. What had occurred hours before had convinced him of this, even if nothing else had.

He'd left Erin in the bedroom and returned to his study, sinking down onto a carpet with a Navajo design he had placed at one side of his desk. He'd acquired it many years during an extended sojourn out West in this country.

Ethan wasn't too egoistic to know when he was over his head. What was it that Kian had said? "The seer sensed a great power emanating from this city." And yes, what else, "The woman you're with is linked somehow to the witch from long ago."

As much as he'd like to ignore him completely, there was something here. He'd seen in Erin's eyes as he'd held her in his arms someone else, someone he once loved profoundly and, in many ways, still did, but also, there was an accompanying darkness.

He prepared himself, settling on the carpet with its swirls and interlocking shades of blues and tans. The Cathars had emphasized the need for meditation and diligently honed their techniques for practicing it — different mindsets and approaches for different goals.

Granted, it was not something he had practiced as much as he should, but he remembered what he'd been taught. Ethan cleared his mind completely. This in itself actually took more than a few moments to achieve as so many divergent forces seemed intent on intruding. But finally, once he reached the particular plateau he sought, he opened himself to guidance in whatever form that might take.

◆

Once his inner sight settled, Ethan slowly became aware of his surroundings. He was inside a cave, not just a cave but, in fact, an enormous cavern. In the distance, he could hear water crashing tumultuously on something. As he changed his focus, he was able to see a cliff outside and jagged rocks below — not serene, surely, but a scene rather more fraught with urgency.

He returned his sight to where he had been, now sitting, deep within the cave whose ceiling and walls were heavily ornamented with dripping white stalactites. It was moist and drafty, and in not too many moments, his complete attention was drawn to a figure who had appeared, standing some yards away from him. Of course, he immediately recognized the garb, the long gray robes. He didn't know why he was surprised, but beyond that, he was intently grateful.

It was undeniably his mentor from his time with the Cathars, Brother Guidrade, who stood before him, smiling kindly. "Etienne, my brother, I have been waiting for you."

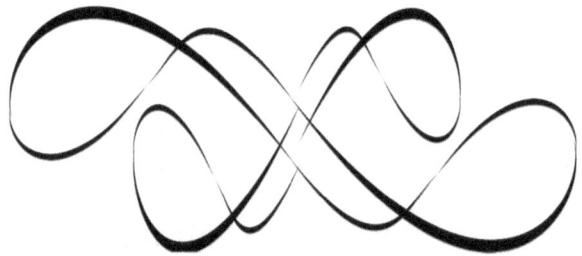

# Chapter 18

# COUNSEL FROM AN OLD FRIEND

They walked silently through the cave. There was so much to say, so much to ask, but he found, oddly, he didn't have it in him. Just being in the presence of his former mentor quieted his soul to an extent. But what was also true was that a distinct sadness had settled in, and he felt intrinsically as though he had failed not one but two women, the two most important to him in his unnaturally long existence. Even though one might consider them the same person in some respects, to Ethan, particularly at this juncture, they felt separate — separate and distinct.

"Your thoughts are shadowed, my Brother," Guidrade spoke softly beside him, breaking the silence that had enveloped them for some time.

"I wonder if I made a mistake coming here, engaging you in this way."

The elderly Cathar Perfect beside him stopped his slow, meandering movement and turned to him. "Much can be learned from mistakes, Etienne, often much more than can be learned from doing things flawlessly."

"Yes, I remember," he replied softly.

"And what else do you remember, Etienne?"

He looked at the wizened face of Brother Guidrade. He was the same as he recalled him from so long ago — always kind, always peaceful, even back then when facing his impending doom. It was truly as though he existed on another level of consciousness where he viewed the foibles of mere mortals or mere immortals with kindness, compassion, and infinite understanding. "I fear, Brother, I have put the ones I love the most in jeopardy. Erin, Erin Holt, I should have stayed away from her. I had no business interfering in her life."

"Was she happy?"

He stopped, jarred a bit, feeling startled at the inquiry, although a seemingly innocuous question. "Happy?"

"Yes, before you reentered her life after you made her forget your existence, do you think she was happy?"

Ethan considered carefully because he knew when a question was received from a Cathar Perfect, it should be given weight. He knew what he'd felt from Erin — from being near her, touching her skin, and being intimate with her. He could feel, yes, so much. Before she arrived in New Orleans, there seemed much dissatisfaction, aimlessness, and, yes, at times, even sadness. "I don't know. I don't suppose I could really say."

His Cathar Brother smiled as though he was more than aware of the truth. "All right, Etienne, let's move to an easier benchmark. Do you think there was peace in her life?"

He bowed his head. Was he here for help or here to reinforce his feelings of guilt? And did he have the luxury of time to do either? "No, no, I do not believe there was peace," he responded quietly.

"You know, Etienne, as much as we'd like to protect another, we cannot protect them from their spiritual path. All spirits who venture to clothe themselves in the flesh and inhabit this world do so for a particular purpose. Not for safety, not for a happy life, but to learn, to learn and perfect the spirit. Even with your extraordinary existence, do not make a mistake in believing you can choose for another. Free will belongs to all souls, even your Erin and your beloved Enid."

"I didn't mean for things to become so complicated."

"You thought this would be simple?" he answered lightly.

He stopped. Did he, did he think at all? "I don't know," he muttered, feeling highly uncomfortable at the intense scrutiny Guidrade was giving this situation. But then again, what had he expected when he reached out for help? This was help, no matter how disturbing it might feel in the moment.

"Yes, well, let's talk for a bit. There may be one or more things I have yet to teach you, my boy, in spite of your age." He gestured to a stone ledge near the entrance of the great cave. Ethan could still hear the water crashing loudly below, outside on the rocks, so turbulent, no doubt highly reflective of his emotional state. "The first thing you must do Etienne is clear your mind. Shed this negativity that is clinging to you."

"It's from the spell," he answered.

"Indeed, but we must be done with it if we are to move forward."

♦

"Mother."

There was silence where there should be none. Ordinarily, the Fairy of the Wildwood would respond to her immediately, as if she were always with her. But not today, today there was a distance she had no understanding of.

"My Lady, have you abandoned me?"

*"That is not possible,"* the whisper wrapped around her, but it was different, removed.

"Why have you changed?"

*"I haven't. I am constant. You have moved further away from me, daughter."* Enid looked down at her hand, tightly grasping the jagged purple stone in her fist. It was one of a group of magical items that the old healer, Bethel, had given her to aid with Geraint's transition. She opened her palm and saw the bright red indentations in her hand, but more than that, she could see clearly that the crystal stone had altered. It had tangibly darkened its tone within her palm, closer to a dark maroon rather than its former lavender tinge.

"I need your help," she murmured with distraction.

*"Yes, I can see that this is so,"* she whispered solemnly. But Enid's gaze was so fixed elsewhere that she couldn't hear the difference in the Lady's tone.

"I have seen through the veil. I have seen another life."

*"That is a dangerous path, my dearest. You should keep your eyes firmly fixed on where you are."*

"But aren't these visions a gift? A new power I am meant to use."

*"Not all power is to be used. Sometimes, the lesson is not to use it."*

"But I have seen Geraint, and he is transformed. Surely, he will welcome me. I have saved him. I am his wife."

The wind wrapped around Enid again, but with a chill that was frightening. *"Dearest, there is much to do here. You know that."*

"It is so difficult. He struggles. He battles with the demon within. He doesn't love me as he used to. He—" and then she hesitated because before now, all of this had been unvoiced. "When he looks at me, he sees the demon in my eyes and hates it."

There was silence now that felt nearly deafening to her. Why had she sought counsel? Why had she reached out? She could act of her own accord. *"You must give him time, time to adjust to this new existence. He does not blame you."*

"No," she whispered. "The Geraint I saw does not blame me. He would not."

*"Enid, do not lose everything seeking what is not yours."*

"How can he not be mine. He will always be mine," she answered.

♦

"Reincarnation is a complicated concept, not nearly as easy to understand as one might think. Within the span of existence, there are a thousand possibilities, a thousand experiences, and for every one chosen, one is not chosen."

"Yes, I understand the divergencies, the probabilities."

They leaned against a shelf of rocks just at the mouth of the enormous cavern. Its ceiling was not low but rather stretched several stories over their heads with a smooth, polished surface that reminded him curiously of onyx. "Understanding and living it are two different things, my friend. Once you reconnected with your soulmate, with Erin, this powerful bond resonated, was felt everywhere."

"Felt? What are you saying?"

"Lifetimes are not lived consecutively. All time exists as one. The present informs the future and the past."

"So, you're saying my wife from long ago, Enid, is aware of what is happening now."

"No, Etienne, I am saying she is being affected by it. You are actively changing the past now. And the woman you once knew is moving in a perilous direction."

"So, then I should stop everything, stop this relationship with Erin."

He shook his head, staring at him a bit grimly now. "It's too late for that my friend. She knows of her, and she covets what she has."

Ethan took a sharp breath, trying to absorb what Guidrade was explaining to him. "That is not the woman I remember. Enid was only ever supportive. She stayed with me even after, after I became cursed."

"Cursed with the wolf?"

"Yes, she did everything to help me, lived for years by my side. I never saw—"

Brother Guidrade bent his head a bit as though listening intently. "Never saw this side of her, and do you remember the man you were back then, my brother?"

Again, the icy water of reality washed over him. "Yes, self-centered, obtuse, and frantic at the calamity that had befallen me."

"Yes, well, good thing you've moved past that stage. Your calamity, the same as misfortune that befalls any living soul, can be a tool for learning. You see, we choose the great events of our lives before birth. How we respond to them, well, that is our free will. But Enid, as I said long ago, she is a powerful individual, so it's crucial she does not fall to, shall we say, darker influences."

He sighed deeply, trying to puzzle a way forward. "And from here, how do I possibly affect her now?"

"Yes, it is complicated, but it might take a further journey, my friend, possibly all the way back to your older self."

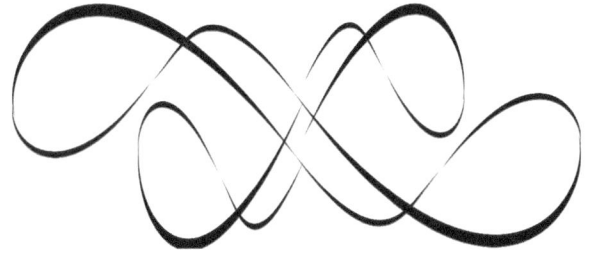

# Chapter 19

# THE LINE

The Line

   In one's life, a line of sorts is always drawn. Some do it at a fairly young age. Others wait until they are older, perhaps their middle years or even later, and then some, of a select few, wait until they are on death's precipice, peering deeply into the unknown void of what is to come. And some don't do it at all. What am I talking about? You might wonder. I am speaking so opaquely about the line we draw and the parameters we sketch concerning what we are willing to accept as possible in our lives, our existence. Again, and let it sink in — what we are willing to accept as possible.

   As a younger man, when I was a man, I had set up those internal boundaries relatively early. I was told that my wife, Enid, might be some sort of enchantress or even a witch with magical capabilities. I listened, but inwardly, I scoffed. I was told my King had been mentored by a wizard. Again, outwardly, I said nothing but dismissed it outright within. Such things did not fit my conception of the world in which I lived and did not fit within the boundaries of what I considered possible. I was, without question, arrogant in my *youth. And nothing cures that particular malady like a bite from a shapeshifter, a lycanthrope, or, if you prefer, a werewolf. What did not fit into my parameter was the fact that now upon every full moon, I would ostensibly transform into a great beast, one that initially struggled to keep its humanity. At times, it almost broke my body in the catastrophic contortions of transformation, and undeniably, it nearly broke my mind as well. Because for me, I became what I had deemed impossible.*

◆

The words of Brother Guidrade seemed to reverberate around the great echoing cavern.

"It might take a further journey, my friend, possibly all the way back to your older self."

They stood there in the quiet together, and Ethan knew that Guidrade would stand there indeed in silence forever, waiting for a response from whomever he was counseling. He remembered well enough from Montségur the infinite well of patience that this particular man possessed.

Ethan sighed wearily in the face of this very daunting proposal. "I can see what you're suggesting, but I have to say I would hope for an easier solution."

"Easier or more palatable?" the old man responded.

"I'm not sure I follow," he said, though, of course, he did.

"I would think it would be a pleasure to reconnect with your former wife again."

"Enid? We have reconnected," he replied a little sharply.

The old man frowned just slightly. "Reincarnation of the spirit does not equal the duplication of someone who has lived before. The spirit is the same, but the soul is different. It is a new life, in many ways a clean slate."

They stopped walking because Ethan was tired of it, tired of them drifting around aimlessly. He took a few short steps to a collection of great stones jutting out from a nearby wall and perched himself up on the flattest one, though it was more slippery than he'd anticipated. Why couldn't Guidrade have made this constructed reality more comfortable? "You had as much to do with this meeting place as I did, Etienne," he answered as though he had heard his thoughts aloud. "Ask," he stated abruptly.

It was clear to Ethan now that interior thoughts were not so interior here. Well, he had opted for guidance in whatever form that might take. "If this is the case, if Erin is indeed a clean slate, why have we reconnected in such a powerful fashion?"

"The relationship between the two of you is one of spirits, not souls. These are deep bonds that remain and link through all lifetimes. If you ceased this existence today and reincarnated, your two spirits would undoubtedly reconnect in subsequent lives. That is how powerful these bonds are. But the personalities and every other nuance that makes a soul unique, that would be altered."

He crossed his arms in front of him. This was not new to him, not a surprise. Ethan had lived a long time. He understood the mechanics of reincarnation, but understanding and living it, well, these were not the same. "So, in many respects, Enid has not returned to me."

He shrugged, "In particulars, no. In essence, possibly. But all of that is not the point, Etienne. The well-being of both of these women is in danger, danger that you have facilitated."

Another uncomfortable truth laid bare. "Yes, I see."

And then the elderly Brother looked at him shrewdly with an expression he well-remembered. "But it seems your reluctance doesn't have as much to do with them as something else, doesn't it, my Brother?"

131

"Yes, I suppose that could be true." This was bothersome. He'd forgotten how the Cathar Perfects had a knack for forcing you to face yourself when it was preferable to keep certain realities at bay.

"Your former self?"

"Indeed, I don't reflect upon him with much satisfaction. He was a different sort of man."

"Of course, so long ago — Medieval times, a fighter, a soldier, an aggressive type of individual."

"A blockhead."

Guidrade smiled indulgently, "I was trying to be kind, as you should be to your former self. You've lived the duration of many, many lifetimes and had much opportunity for choice, for evolution. In the span of your existence, you might consider him the child and you the adult."

"An unruly child, I wonder, at times, how she could bear to love me at all."

"Enid? Well, in many ways, she was a product of her time as well. You might consider that when—" Suddenly, his voice faded away.

Ethan looked up at him and said pointedly. "You were going to say when I see her again."

Once more, that elusive smile as though Guidrade was somewhat proud of him in some inexplicable regard. "Very good. You're beginning to catch on to this place."

"But going back, how would I function? How would I exist, and what would happen to my former self? And what could I possibly do to help the situation now?"

He nodded, "All good questions that I suppose you'll have to figure out as you go."

"And how long—"

"Would you stay? Again unknown, this is your path, Etienne. You have to be the one to accept it. But I must warn you. Time is running short. Even now, some are closing in to take advantage of this turbulent situation."

"Erin?"

"Safe for now, but your former acquaintances, well, for lack of a better description, smell power in the air."

He felt a coldness wrap around him as the image of Kian and even Lapetus crossed his mind. How far would they go? He wondered. "I see the time for deliberation is over."

"It seems so, my Brother."

He pushed off the rock, standing up. "How do I proceed?"

"As always, one small step at a time."

♦

Pain, pain does unrelenting things to the mind, to the heart. When Enid was a young girl, she felt peace. She wandered amongst the trees in the dense forest beyond her home without fear, feeling purely a part of the infinite whole.

But then the visions began to come when she was just past her thirteenth birthday. "What is this darkness that is approaching?"

*"Do not let fear take root in you, little one. It will spread like the wildest vine, entangling and suffocating everything it touches."* She would counsel her, the Fairy of the Wildwood. Only years later, she would admit to Enid that she was the spirit of her true mother.

"Can I be where you are?"

*"Not yet, little one. You have a full life to lead."*

"But the future frightens me. I want to be safe where you are."

*"Do not be afraid of the days ahead. We all go through difficult times. It is the path of the spirit, and you are not just flesh but spirit as well."*

And so, she accepted, as was her nature back then. She lived a quiet life with her father and stepmother. But always returned to the forest until that one day when she sat on the edge of the earth with her bare feet dangling in the water. She had laid back on the banks of the stream with her eyes closed, allowing herself to simply be and connect with every living thing around her, allowing her spirit to drink deeply of the peace of the natural forest. So deeply enmeshed was she that she didn't hear his approach until he was there, standing beside a tree across the babbling creek.

She jolted when her senses understood that she was not alone. Sitting up abruptly, initial shock overtook her at the sight of the golden man clothed in his tarnished armor, looking at her with an interest in his eyes that she did not yet understand as she'd been raised in so much innocence.

"Well," he said, smiling. "What have we here?"

And she felt it just being in his presence — powerful like a dagger being lodged into her heart. But it wasn't a dagger exactly as one would expect. It burrowed deep, invisibly, and there was pain, not because it had injured her but because it had changed who she was.

♦

Enid awoke in the darkened bedroom. The dream still clung to her or was it simply a memory couched in the trappings of a dream? The room was shrouded in shadows, with only cascading ribbons of light here and there sneaking beneath the great wooden door and the tapestries blocking out the moonlight.

For a moment, her heart clutched. Moonlight, had she forgotten? Was this the cycle of the full moon? She hadn't taken precautions for Geraint. Could she have been so thoughtless to

134

have lost track of time? But then she stilled herself, clutching her chest that was filled with pain caused by sheer panic. No, no, the fog cleared. They weren't in the cycle yet, another fortnight at least. She tried to still her breathing. She had to be calm and think clearly.

But as she looked beside her in the darkness, she saw the spot on the bed empty. Where was Geraint?

Again, she peered about the great chamber. The wooden door well beyond the foot of the bed was closed. Where had he gone? It was not like him to leave in the middle of the night. He rested heavily. He was so tired since, since the wolf had begun to take hold.

And then she heard a slight movement across the room in front of one of the tapestries covering a far window. She pulled the covers tightly up around her nightgown. She still couldn't quite see through the blackness.

She heard a voice, a quiet voice. "Be still, my wife. I am here."

"Geraint," she whispered with surprise. "Why are you sitting alone in the shadows?"

"Thinking, love."

And then she heard movement, and a candle was suddenly lit on the table beside him. Ghostly, his face seemed pale next to the flickering light, as though life had been drained out of it. "Are you ill, my husband?"

"That is a question. But I have been considering, watching closely, and weighing matters profoundly these last few days."

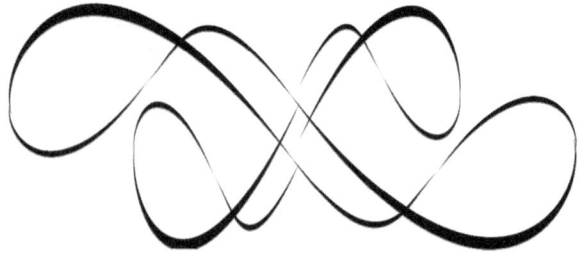

Chapter 20

# ANEIRA

T ime

   This one is a difficult concept, depending upon who you
ask. The philosophy of the Cathars at Montsegur provides a
rather simple yet problematic interpretation of the notion of time.
According to these wise people, time is purely an illusion. For them,
life itself on earth and elsewhere perhaps is simply an imagined sort
of episode designed by the spirit for learning, evolving their nature.
This self-constructed "play" of imagination is lived out, considered
reality by its participants, and then ends, at which point the person
in question "dies" and awakes to his real life, actual reality. So, all
concepts of linear time are simply self-imposed constructs, boundaries if you will, to help give order to this imagined existence. This is
how it is possible for one day to stretch on endlessly, packed with
significant events and for weeks, to fly by with little consequence.
And if one recognizes this truth, truly embraces it, then breaking
those artificial barriers becomes possible. In fact, all sorts of things
and intriguing variations become possible.

*Difficult to wrap one's mind around? Indeed, for most, it is easier and less demanding to embrace the dream.*

♦

### 3 Days Before

When he awoke, astonishingly he found himself in a forest beside a jewel-blue stream. The sun was warm on his face as though he'd fallen asleep by the banks of the babbling water. At the initial sight of his environment, Ethan couldn't help but be overwhelmed by the profound sadness gripping him. This place he remembered well from long ago when he was a boy — a boy playing with no care or knowledge of how dark the world could be.

*"Don't dwell in those places, or you won't be of use to anyone."*

He sat up from the reclining position he'd had on the moist grass. Noting for the first time, he was dressed in the appropriate long gray jacket and maroon-colored doublet beneath atop his dark gray breeches from that time long ago, he looked around sharply, but there was nothing, no one. "Who is this?" he spoke with aggravation.

*"That's true. We've never met, although I was your wife's constant companion for most of her days."*

Again, Ethan attempted to focus on his surroundings and, in doing so, found that his head was pounding. Odd for him, as his existence as a lycanthrope usually kept him in good physical condition. *"It's a stress, even for you attempting to be conscious in two different physical spaces simultaneously. You might consider relinquishing one for a while."*

He rubbed his eyes as he had to admit he felt disoriented. "I don't like taking advice from a disembodied voice, Aneira."

Again, he looked up, but this time, he saw something different. A young woman stood across the stream from him, dressed in a long white flowing dress of what he believed was samite. *"Enid calls me the Lady of the Wildwood."*

He leaned back on his hands, studying the young woman, younger even than his physical age. Her hair was long, thick, and dark, not blond like Enid, and her eyes pure green like the forest. But he could still see some resemblance between mother and daughter in bone structure and expression. "Why are you here?"

She stared at him serenely, actually speaking aloud. "I'm here to help, Etienne."

"Etienne not Geraint," he murmured.

She smiled serenely. "I need to distinguish between the two of you. And as a matter of course, Geraint was never very receptive to my guidance. But you, you are a different matter."

He stretched, profoundly feeling the aches and fatigue, "I'm too am here to help," he said flatly, though he doubted profoundly whether there was any chance of success in this.

"Selfless, how novel. Men of this era found it quite difficult to separate self-interests from their quests."

He nodded slowly, "Yes, it was undeniably a different time. Though there were some able to better themselves through trials."

She smiled again softly, and he decided in that instant that he liked her. "That's true. Your King's knights were sent places far and wide to improve their natures. So, tell me, Etienne, what is your noble quest?"

He took in a breath that, instead of soothing, felt uncomfortable, as though a blade had lodged somewhere around his lungs. "I am here to help Enid."

Her eyes narrowed slightly as she stared at him unflinchingly. "Yes, I can see you believe that. But be sure you are here to help her and not simply to ensure she doesn't interfere with your new life."

"My new life?" he asked with concern.

"With the girl, the auburn-haired one in the other place."

Her forthrightness startled him. "I am concerned about them both," he said with irritation, not liking his motives to be questioned by one who, at least in appearance, seemed so young.

"Yes," she answered softly. "Then, if you wish, I will help you, Etienne."

Again, he felt an uncomfortable pain in his chest, and a thought occurred to him. "Where is Geraint? The man I was now."

"At present? He is resting but not amicably, as you probably already sense. He fights what he does not understand. Just as he fights the transformation into the wolf."

"Enid keeps it from me," then he corrected himself, "from him."

She crouched down a bit, delicately sitting down on the banks of the stream across from him as though she was settling in for a casual chat. "Yes, she takes much upon herself. That is part of the problem, her profound love for you. At present, Enid is ruled by fear. Fear makes people take desperate measures at times. And, of course, she is being influenced."

"Influenced? By who?" He snapped angrily. He stopped himself, feeling an odd stirring within.

She frowned ever so slightly, but not enough to mar her lovely face. "Yes, you should be careful of that, Etienne. Wild, primitive emotions could stir him. Then you'll be battling more than you bargained for. So, where were we?" she asked gently.

"You said Enid was being influenced."

"Yes, I did. And that is something you should consider. Who would hold sway over your lovely wife?"

"Why do you ask if you know the answer?"

"I do know, Etienne. But I'm not here to take your quest from you. This is your path. You're not too old to learn a few new things."

He grimaced. It was true. He felt the pull to lower emotions, lower energy vibrations as Brother Guidrade would call them. "Then, why are you here again, Aneira?"

"To be a friendly ear, Etienne, provide support, give you someone to talk to, perhaps."

"I'm not a green child, you know."

She inclined her head to the side, looking at him almost quizzically, "I do. But I am heartened that you are willing to try Etienne. And for that, I commend you and might mention that there is a woman, an old woman who purports to be a healer that supplies Enid with the means to subdue you during the moon's cycle."

He considered, "A woman? I don't remember anyone."

"No, no, you wouldn't," she said almost dismissively. "Again, you were concerned with your pursuits at this time. Much went by you, I might say. Much, indeed."

Decidedly, he stood up, dusting himself off of debris from the grass. "How much time do you estimate I have?"

She echoed his actions, coming to her feet as well. "Time? Well, that is the matter, is it not? If I were you, I would move quickly. Our friend will not slumber forever. And it wouldn't do for you two to be battling for one body."

◆

It was early Spring. He recalled the feeling in the air, able to mark the passing of the seasons by their solid predictability. The breeze still felt cool, but as the day passed, the sun's warmth began to bleed through the air. He'd forgotten, or perhaps he'd buried it.

Ethan walked quickly along the pathway through the forest. He could tell by the amount of light that it was late afternoon. Once he reached the edge of the woods, he paused, catching his breath. Not far on the crest of a hill was his father's castle. It brought pain to him, the sight, more than he had anticipated. It had been so long, so long, so many mortal lifespans. And he questioned deeply at this moment what he had indeed learned beyond how to survive such an existence. And now, unbelievably, here he was, just as though everything had begun again.

"Be careful, Etienne. Don't be distracted from your purpose." Suddenly, the dark-haired fae woman was standing next to him, where there had been no one moments before.

"Erin," he murmured, a vision of her rising in his mind. "Is she all right?"

"Yes, for now. But things are unstable. You must focus. Do not let the past overtake your resolve."

"I still don't understand how I can affect what has been."

She looked at him with a wise expression, clearly too wise for such a young face. "How can I stand before you now, Etienne, in the flush of my youth?"

"Because you're no longer of this world."

She laughed, "How can someone as old as you have learned so little? I am as much of this world as you are and am part of other worlds as well. I have only shed the flesh that you earth-bound ones prize so much. Time is one, Etienne. Don't let rigidness confine your thought."

"I would not be here if that were so." He breathed in deeply, the sweet air of the early Spring, and then steeled himself. "The woman."

"Yes, she calls herself a healer," Aneira spoke with a light tint of sarcasm that another might have missed.

He looked at her oddly, "And that is not what you call her, my Lady of the Wildwood?"

She smiled, seemingly pleased with his deference. "No, Etienne, I call her a witch in its worst manifestation."

"Where will I find her?"

"Surely, not in your father's castle but in the village. Enid has procured a cottage for her there, convinced she still needs her services."

"All right," he said, trying again to remember how inconspicuously to get to the stables.

The Lady of the Wildwood smiled again as if all of this were some amusement for her. And then she pointed, "That way, Etienne, Godspeed."

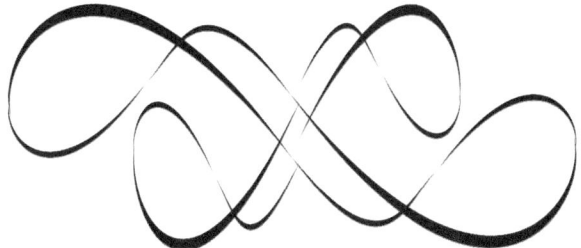

# Chapter 21

# BETHEL

I t was not raining, but it felt as though it was. She could feel the sharp pains stretching between her shoulder blades then scissoring down her spine. As a young girl, she'd been kicked in the spine harshly by a nobleman in her village, then dragged off and used violently for his distorted pleasure. Since then, it had always been a vulnerable spot.

Bethel watched the candle on the windowsill flicker wildly, though there was no breeze to influence it. Something was coming. She looked about the small room of her cottage for her woolen wrap to wrap around her well-worn gray tunic. She should leave and let whatever was on its way pass. But she ached so, and she was tired, tired of dodging the whims of others, the Lady of the castle, the dark ones from the other side of the forest — Lapetus and his cohort Kian. She was not yet in her seventieth year but felt like an old woman.

So, instead, she sat in the rocking chair near the unlit fireplace and sipped the tea she had brewed.

She needed vitality. That was the rub of it. Practitioners of the arts depleted themselves in ways that others did not understand. The blond one, Lady Enid, was not so easy to pull from now. Initially, Bethel took much life force from her, but she had passed through some doorway that Bethel had not foreseen.

She really hadn't expected the husband to survive, but he had. And her Lady had brought her here to aid her. Yes, she lived on the scraps of vitality that she could find to pull from various sources, but it was only surviving. She believed in coming here that she would do better.

Moving painfully, she tried to stretch out her aching back while continuing to sip the steaming mug. Someone was coming. She could feel the fall of a horse's hoofbeats pounding the ground. The sight showed her the white stallion, but the rider was obscured, a stranger to her.

She thought of the nobleman who had beaten and raped her when she was only a child. Years later, she sought him out when he had aged, an older man. She had blended in the crowd and first added the herb to his unattended mug of ale. Once she spied its effects on him, simulating drunkenness, she moved seamlessly behind him when he was surrounded by a throng of peasants from the village.

He was laughing when she plunged the long, spindly dagger into his back, just between the shoulder blades where he'd kicked her. The herb had numbed him, so there was no pain, no crying out. It was not noticed; she was certain until she was disappearing down a wooded path. She felt the rush of vitality from her when he perished. It drained her for months, but she considered it well worth her effort.

A powerful knock at the door jolted her out of her reminiscence.

Bethel considered at that moment that she should have left. She quietly waited. Perhaps it would pass, and whoever it was would leave. The candle's flame on the windowsill still curiously danced, heralding chaos, perhaps peril.

She would be silent as she had been as a child, hoping she would not be noticed.

She daredn't breathe, but back then, it was to no avail. She was dragged out, dragged out of her hiding place, dragged into the dust.

She waited, but there was no sound. Perhaps this time, all danger would pass over her, and she would escape unscathed.

But then, a mighty crash and her door splintered as it was kicked open. She didn't stir, just watched. The face was familiar, but the soul altered dramatically.

♦

Ethan hadn't approached the castle, only the stables, wishing to put off any contact with Enid until necessary. Oddly, he felt in his blood that before he saw her again, he needed to be prepared.

But joyfully, in the stables, he did find an old comrade to reunite with, Uasail, his beloved horse. Although the grooms seemed unfazed by his presence, his horse was another matter. The great snow-colored stallion seemed suspicious, begrudgingly accepting, but also confused, as though he sensed the change on some level. Ethan fed him an apple he'd picked from a nearby grove, hopeful to meet his old friend. It was a peace offering that was accepted, albeit somewhat reluctantly.

"My Lord, Lady Enid was asking after you when I saw her in the Great Hall."

The young man whose name eluded him at the moment was smiling. Ethan answered with authority, "Tell her I have business to attend to. I'll return later." And then quickly, he rode off, trying to shake the feeling of anxiety that seemed determined to cling to him as he rode toward the village.

*"Focus, Etienne,"* Aneira whispered in his mind as he traveled the well-trodden road. It was true the emotions of being back here were nearly paralyzing. Would he have chosen to go forward if he knew where his life would go? He couldn't help but wonder. There were so many lonely years he'd spent filling up time with often empty events after, after Enid's death. But it was her. He had to remember he was here for her now. "Yes," Was the answer, the softest whisper on the breeze.

As he led Uasail to the edge of the village, he considered how he would locate the old woman's cottage. *"Her dwelling borders the edge of the forest, not too close for neighbors to see what dark ceremonies occupy her."* He cleared his mind to try to visualize where that would be in his recollections of the area, but an exact location rose in his mind. Clearly, Aneira was more invested in the outcome here than she let on. And, of course, he had forgotten that this land at this time was more welcoming of magic than the modern world would ever be.

◆

They had never exchanged a word, but she knew him. She knew him when he was ill and laid hands on him to tether his spirit to this world. She knew him when she placed his young wife's palms atop his wound and allowed her to drink in the darkness from the wolf's clan. And he had never acknowledged her, not even when he regained consciousness.

At that moment, she had decided to take what she could for herself of this dire situation. The next time she saw Enid, she drank deeply from her, weakening her resistance to the shadows. And then again, each time she could, until the young one stopped her. It was power. Power Bethel had not suspected Lady Enid possessed.

With difficulty, the old woman came to her feet. Her bones cramped with pain that none of her remedies felt inclined to relieve. "My Lord, forgive me. I'd fallen asleep and did not hear your knock." She eyed the splintered wood where he'd forced the door, wondering if he would even offer to replace it.

He crossed into the shadowed room, and she felt a chill accompany him. She knew he was infected with lycanthropy, but she'd never felt this from him before, this emanation of, dare she name it, malevolence.

He eyed her oddly as though he did not know her. "What do you call yourself?"

She swallowed on a dry throat, looking around. There was nothing close to her to grab to protect herself. "Bethel, my Lord, I serve your wife, Lady Enid, as a healer."

He moved closer to her, and she felt genuine concern because deep within his blue-gray eyes, she saw something she didn't understand. She saw cunning that she had never seen in him before. "Do you, Bethel? And tell me quickly, who else do you serve?"

Instinctively, she skirted around the small wooden table that held bowls filled with herbs from her new garden. "I-I do not understand what you mean, my liege. I only serve—"

He slapped the table before her, throwing it across the cottage until it slammed against the wall. "Do not lie to me, old woman. What have you done to my wife?"

She'd had dreams of it often enough. All who dabbled in the Arts for good or ill were allowed a glimpse into their fate. Hers would be quick but also savage. And sadly, it would be well-deserved. "To Lady Enid? I-I only tried to help her. She wanted to stop, to stop—" She hesitated. She did not know how much he knew, how much his young wife had been able to conceal from him.

"To stop the wolf?" he said in a low, dangerous voice.

He knew. Her heart sank as she racked her brain, trying to find something to bargain with. "Yes, yes, forgive me, my Lord.

They forced me, forced me to include it," she mumbled tearfully. It was the best hope, her only course to beg for sympathy.

He moved closer to her, and she could smell it in her nostrils, the beast stirring. But it could not be. There was no moon. It was only late afternoon. "Forced you to do what, Bethel?"

"The one of your clan, Lapetus. I included the poison in the mixture I gave Enid to stop the transformation."

And then he was upon her, his hands grabbing her frail bones so tightly, so painfully, she was sure they would snap under the pressure. "What does it do, Bethel?"

Oh no, she felt it washing over her, the anger coursing from him into her aged body. It was him. He would be the chosen instrument of her karma. He would be her undoing. As he shook her violently, she shuddered. "It will drive whoever touches it to madness," she rasped brokenly.

"Do you mean me?" he said with white, piercing anger.

She shook her head frantically, "No, the wolf protects you. But not Enid. They wanted her gone. She stands between you." He released her abruptly and walked across the room, staring into the fireplace she'd just lit a short time ago. The day was not chilled, but she felt an iciness in her veins always, always so cold. She stared at him with disbelief. It made no sense. He had the look of Geraint, but something was wrong. "What, are you a demon? I see the past and the future in your eyes. How can this be?" She murmured almost to herself.

And then he turned around, staring at her with a cold expression. "What am I to do with her?" he murmured.

And Bethel heard the voice, a clear, pure voice that seemed to be everywhere. *"The old woman is dying from her own sins. It would be a mercy to relieve her of her suffering."*

She remembered as a young woman plunging that sharp blade into his shoulders. And Bethel remembered believing this would be the beginning of her life, not understanding that it was actually the end. The hand that connected with her throat was clawed, like an animal, and the twist was swift and complete with only a quick snap.

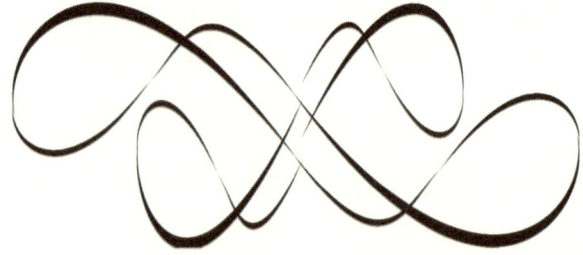

# Chapter 22

# KILLING

K illing

    *Have I killed? Yes, more than a few times. I began my career as a military sort, a knight, a warrior, a soldier, and then later a mercenary. And yes, I was a priest at one time, and some might argue that I killed a few souls in the process. Of course, there were many at the beginning of my metamorphosis or some might term when I was "cursed," though I might argue with that description. The Cathars taught that all momentous events in one's life are not by chance but rather selected before birth, when you are between lives floating about without the physical/earthly body. Selected for what purpose, you might ask.*

    *To them, everything is a tool for learning.*

    *Thus, if you are afflicted by a disease, it is to learn from.*

    *If you marry someone unsuitable to you, it is to learn from.*

    *If you are bitten by a lycanthrope and doomed to a restless immortality, that too is to learn from.*

*Now, how you react to all these situations is Free Will. You choose the reaction and thus choose the consequences.*

*I remember long ago, before the siege at Montsegur and the genocide of the Cathars when Brother Guidrade and I were sitting out on a plateau looking out over the Pyrenees. As I recall, I asked him what the consequences of my history of killing could be.*

*He seemed to consider before he answered as was his way. Initially, I thought my good brother was just slow to speak, but in retrospect, I understood that perhaps he was obtaining guidance from another more spiritual source before he responded.*

*"Yes, Etienne, there is no doubt your violent history has led to troubling consequences for you. Taking another life takes a toll on a spirit that, if it can be overcome, takes quite some time. In effect, when you interfere with a natural demise, you are trying to usurp the creator's place. But, of course, circumstances are paramount. Death on a battlefield, self-defense is not the same as willful murder."*

*"Yes," I remember answering. "I have to say that I have done both."*

*Back then, I remember he seemed unaffected by my response. He continued to gaze serenely out at the breathtaking vista before us. "And you have suffered for it, Etienne."*

*And he was right. There was always a price or a consequence, as more spiritually minded individuals would like to describe. But for myself, I called it a price.*

♦

Ethan left the village after his confrontation with Bethel. Once he'd snapped her neck, he gently placed her in the bed, covering her body with a blanket. He then set the disarray in the cottage as closely back to its original state as he could. He didn't precisely fear repercussions. He was King in this vicinity now that his father had passed on to his great reward. No one would question his decisions. However unjust they might be. But as the man he was, the modern incarnation of Geraint, it troubled him.

The woman had a dark soul, of that, he had no doubt. She was pushing his wife, Enid, toward a similar path, but time and long life had shown him nuances in every form of living. And he questioned his decision in a way that he would not have done so in his youth.

*"Do not spend too much time on this, Etienne. As I said, she was infirmed and would have died soon enough anyway."* It was Aneira's voice in his mind again. She was becoming quite comfortable usurping his conscience.

"I am not comfortable killing for expediency, my Lady," he muttered.

"Yes, well, try to remember where you are, Etienne. Your hesitation here could be the end of you. These are different times. Men are ruled by their passions, not intellect. They have not yet evolved their higher natures."

"Barbaric times," he muttered.

"Yes, I suppose, to you now, that would seem so."

◆

"Lady," she heard the whisper. But there was only silence and then a scream, a scream that clawed and clenched at her heart. "Enid," it screeched in horror and then silence.

Enid opened her eyes. She trembled as she canvassed her bedchamber, where she had come to collect her thoughts. Just that morning, she'd felt something, something unsettling, shifting around her. She'd reached out to the Lady of the Wildwood, her eternal guide, but there was nothing, just quiet.

This unease had clung to her all day and then, into the afternoon. Her first thought was that something was amiss with Geraint, so she asked to have him fetched to her. But he did not come, not even when he'd finished his daily appointments and activities. He did not come.

It was odd, usually he was quite attentive, though erratic, especially since he'd become one with the wolf. Unconsciously, she felt he'd even become dependent on her as she ostensibly controlled his transformation. But not today. Something shifted, and she sensed separation from him.

Confused, she'd retired here, lit a candle, and tried to reach out to identify what was occurring. First, she again attempted to contact the Fairy of the Wildwood for counsel, but she was only met with silence.

It wasn't all that astonishing. There had been a break between them as of late. And Enid blamed herself. Her Lady did not approve of decisions she'd made lately. She had encouraged Enid to be more open with Geraint about his condition, but she feared that he would not be able to live with it. She feared deeply that he would choose instead not to go on and leave her alone.

She took a sharp breath within. That was it. That was the unacknowledged fear that she'd carried lodged within her heart. All would be well if she could manage things with Bethel's help. They could live as peaceful a life as possible as long, and a distinct chill swept up her spine, as long as she could keep the others away — the dark clan that had done this to him.

And for this, she needed power.

She breathed in deeply and focused, focused on the other one, the witch as Bethel had called her. "Take what you need from her, my Lady. There is a connection there, and you can pull."

She focused, allowing every other thought to drop away. *"Enid,"* a whisper, a tendril, and she knew it was the Fairy of the Wildwood trying to dissuade her, but she pushed it aside. She would protect what was hers.

Her mind was powerful — this she knew even when she was a child wandering the forest. Everyone thought she was so amiable, so kind, so easily bent to their will. Even her love, Geraint, did not see her for who she truly was. So, she allowed him and everyone else to believe what they wanted.

The power of her focus was like a great directed arrow that pierced and burrowed through layers of the veil until she found what she sought.

The woman was asleep in a room whose attributes faded away at her intensity. All she saw was her. Sleep was good. She had often led her away during sleep to a place where she was vulnerable.

Enid focused, intent on entering her dreams, but something stopped her. She felt it acutely, painfully, as though she'd crashed into an invisible wall.

"What sorcery is this?" she muttered angrily beneath her breath. Again, she tried to pierce the impediment, but something stopped her, something so strong. Someone knew, knew what she was doing.

Again, she drew deeply on her power within, focusing intently. She would not be stopped. And just before, before she launched her assault.

She heard the terrified scream in her mind raking across her heart and pulling ruthlessly from her store of power until it faded and dissipated into silence.

Enid opened her eyes, trembling uncontrollably. She was completely depleted. The vision of the other girl was gone, and she had no power left to reach her.

She sank into a chair in the corner of the great chamber, still shaking without even the strength to rise, her legs trembling. Her mind also trembled within because she knew. She knew the voice. It was Bethel, Bethel's scream and terror that had ripped through her, Bethel who had torn her power away from her.

Enid sat mutely in the chair, feeling like a shell. She couldn't see or tell what had occurred. She continued to breathe deeply, so shaken. What was she to do now? How would she recover?

Everything began to fold in upon itself, and she remained there, sitting immobile. Moments passed, perhaps longer, perhaps much longer. She had no idea how much time. And then suddenly, the great wooden door of her bedchamber swept open. Even her vision was hazy, but she saw a figure standing in the doorway, motionless, just looking at her.

Her first thought was fear because she did not recognize this man.

"Who are you?" her voice croaked like an old woman's.

And then he moved within the room, approaching her, not stopping until he stood before her. "Don't you recognize me, my Lady? It is I, Geraint, your husband."

Enid took a quick breath. Yes, the features and the clothing were the same. And there was a familiarity, but something she could not mark clearly was changed. "Yes," she said softly. "I see you now."

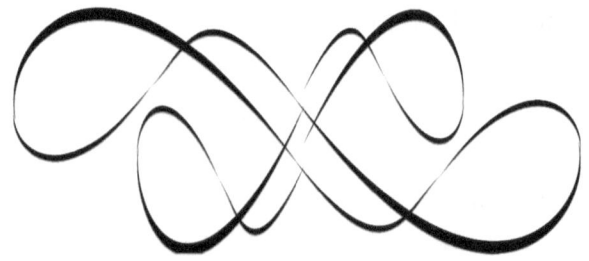

# THE DIFFERENCE

"She's going to know the difference."

*"You are Geraint, granted a different Geraint, but still her husband."*

"Lady, I don't have the time to debate this. But if Enid has become as powerful as you have indicated, she will know."

There was silence, but he could still feel the presence of Aneira near him. Clearly, she hadn't considered this facet of things. Ethan was moving through the great hall of the castle slowly. Any moment, he could happen upon his beautiful, young, and potentially treacherous wife, and his cover could be blown.

The idea of aligning the description of treacherous with lovely Enid truly confounded him. He could not match his memory of her at all with that idea. In fact, the thought angered him greatly, not especially at her but at himself, his obtuseness for a better word.

"*It is a different time,*" was the lightest murmur. "*Guard your feelings, Etienne. Too many primal emotions could wake the sleeping one.*"

That's right, for the moment, he'd forgotten he was in a borrowed body, and all of this was his mess to deal with.

Then, quickly on the heels of that thought Aneira interjected, "*All right, I have found a solution, albeit a temporary one. I've woven a spell, a veil over you. Enid will find it confusing but will believe the difficulty is with her. It seems the death of Bethel cost her greatly.*"

Ethan nodded to two young pages passing through the main gallery. He stopped and gazed around, wrestling with such strong, conflicting impulses connected with being in his boyhood home again. "*Focus,*" she whispered with strength.

He turned to head up the heavy stone staircase. "Aneira, I have no plan, no idea how to help now."

"*I know. That you must discover as you go along,*" she answered as he began to take the massive steps upward.

"You said the old witch damaged Enid."

"*She tore away much lifeforce from Enid in her death. She'd gotten her claws into your wife before she died.*"

"I am sorry to hear that," he said softly. "It seems I didn't know my spouse nearly as well as I thought I did."

"*Indeed.*"

He hesitated on the threshold, feeling completely overcome. A rush of a thousand memories flooded in, memories that he'd not only forgotten but that he'd entombed. In some ways, he could count the time he'd spent here with this woman as the sweetest, most precious era of his life.

And in that moment, a cascade of strong emotions flooded in, momentarily overwhelming, including possessiveness, jealousy, determination, and desire. He knew, without question, he was battling that other part of him that was asleep.

"*Steady,*" he heard the whisper of Aneira.

◆

He could see his wife — Enid, across the chamber sitting near a candle that was lit. Much was shadowed, most of her form. Ethan concentrated, trying to focus. He was here to help, to stop her from making severe errors in judgment.

He waited, waited for her to make the first move. And it felt interminable. His instinct was to rush in and take charge. That was what he would have done in the past. It took all his self-control just to stay there and not move.

Finally, he heard her voice, which seemed shaky and uncertain. "Who are you?" she asked.

"*Go to her,*" Aneira's coaxing, and that was all it took. Enid was still his responsibility. He moved into the room until he stood directly in front of her. Finally, in the candlelight, he could make out her lovely features. For a moment, it seemed as though his heart had ceased beating, so overwhelmed was he in seeing her again in the flesh. He had forgotten, or perhaps he had blocked how truly exquisite she was in her long, flowing, burgundy-colored gown. But those eyes, those lovely amber eyes, had darkened somehow, less filled with light than he remembered and gazing at him with confusion.

"*Reassure her,*" Aneira instructed.

"Don't you recognize me, my Lady? It is I, Geraint. Your husband." He spoke softly but with confidence. It was important she believe.

And then she murmured softly, "Yes, I see you now."

She did not smile at him. He remembered her smile when he danced with her on their wedding day at the court of his King. On their wedding night, hers was a smile that would have lit a thousand kingdoms. But now, he recalled painfully, when he asked her for her hand in marriage, there was no smile but something else in her eyes.

What had she said then? He could scarcely remember. He had been so intent on what he wanted. He had disregarded her father's trepidation. And he had disregarded her fear that came back to him as clearly as a pure bell ringing across time. "I hesitate, my lord. I am not sure I am the kind of woman who can make you happy."

"Enid," he sighed deeply, so much that it was not unnoticed by his wife. "Forgive me."

He heard her take a sharp breath inward. That's right. That was not his way, admitting fault. Even back then, when he'd misjudged her and accused her of disloyalty, he could not admit his fault. And she had always understood quietly and with unwavering support, or rather she seemed to have understood. "Forgive you? For what, my husband?" she answered quietly.

*"Don't make a muddle of this, Etienne. You are not here to live happily ever after. You are here to solidify a place for your former self."*

It felt like a stab, her words. He wanted, well, he wanted to make amends. He wanted to make her happy. Was that so terrible?

*"Enid is not for you,"* she reminded him. *"She is for him."*

"But I am him," he sent the thought out strongly. She was still his wife.

*"Are you, though?"* Aneira asked indulgently. *"Would you abandon that poor sweet soul in the future? Erin Holt, Enid's future incarnation. Would you leave her in exchange for staying here and reliving these times? And if you did, what would you leave her vulnerable to?"*

A stab of concern flooded over him at her chilling words. "What does that mean?"

*"It means you cannot have it both ways. If you are here, he is there. What kind of man could he be in your world?"*

"You speak in riddles. We are the same."

*"No, no, Etienne, you have learned much and evolved in ways you have not even considered, and this world is raw and filled with magic."*

He looked more deeply into Enid's eyes. He could feel much. She was confused, so confused. And then he understood — energy, lifeforce. The witch had drained her so deeply before she died.

He held out his hand for her. "Wife," he murmured.

Enid looked at his hand hesitantly but then gingerly put her hand in his grasp. Almost aggressively, he pulled her forcibly to her feet. The brown eyes gazed at him with surprise but seemed to clear a bit. What was true was that between soulmates, intimacy could generate a considerable amount of energy, and energy was clearly what his wife needed at the moment. "I've missed you," he said with steel in his voice before he pulled her inward for an embrace.

He felt the confusion in her and resistance, but Ethan bent to kiss her, kiss Enid as he'd done a thousand times more than a thousand years ago. At first, she seemed frightened, trying to puzzle out the difference, and then she acquiesced and melted in his embrace. The kiss was passionate, desperate, he might say. There would only be so many times now that he could do this, only so many times that they could be together. Out of pure selfishness, he would savor it.

He swept her up in his arms, carrying her to the bed.

"I don't understand," she whispered, but he kissed her again, drowning out all her concerns in his determined passion.

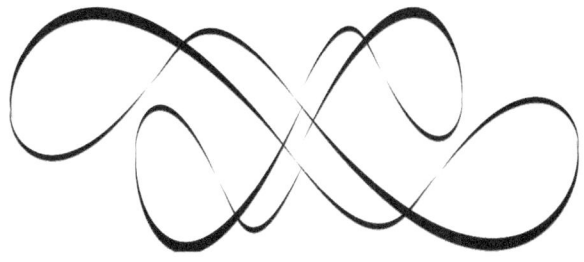

# Chapter 24

# THE EDGE OF A DARK FOREST

"*Lady,*" this time, it was a hushed whisper in her mind muffled out by the sound of her husband's breathing. She glanced over to him beside her, lying in bed. He was asleep, so tired. She felt his exhaustion emanating from him so clearly.

But why?

Quietly, she sat up in the massive bed, pulling the blankets securely around her.

He had been so gentle with her but passionate. And she could feel without question that he intended to comfort and reassure her. It was tender, his loving, and all was well. He wanted her to know, to believe that.

"*Lady*," it whispered throughout the chamber, and she felt a stab in her heart at the sound. All was well. He wanted her to believe.

She passed her hand quietly over his chest without touching it and focused. She could see a particular red glow permeating from him. Enid drew in a sharp breath. It was clear now. He had killed. She could see the evidence in his life force and had killed not long before he came to her. She swallowed on a fearful throat. He was deceiving her.

And then his eyes opened, and he smiled. "Enid," he murmured. Again, his arms went around her, and he pulled her against him.

◆

He dreamed that he walked on the edge of a dark forest.

"You don't belong here."

It was a man's voice that he heard, somewhat fierce, determined, but laced with something nearly imperceptible, imperceptible that was to everyone else but him.

"What are you going on about?"

Then he turned around, having pinpointed the location. The speaker was sitting on the edge of a grassy hill — the one poised just before the menacing forest. One spill and you could easily roll into its vines and branches and be engulfed in that tangled mess.

He smiled with menace back at him. "Are you sure that tangled mess isn't the life you left behind?"

He frowned. Now Ethan really hadn't expected this.

"I'm trying to help," he muttered.

"Help, yes, help indeed, by sleeping with my wife. If we were in the flesh right now, I'd slice you to pieces, then burn what was left over the hottest fire that my vassals could manage."

"You should be resting," he said calmly because reason, he was sure, wouldn't be much help here.

"Rest? With all this going on behind my back?"

"Don't blame Enid," he said hesitantly, crossing his arms. These spiritual excursions were getting more than a bit taxing to him.

His former self eyed him with disdain. So odd, his manner, his carriage was completely different. Oh yes, of course, arrogance or perhaps pride. Now, he remembered how pride played such a part in all the mishaps Geraint used to get himself into.

His former self frowned, "Again, old man, what are you going on about?"

Old man? Now that stung, coming out of his younger version's mouth. He glanced down at the shadowed trees clustering at the foot of the green hill. This was undeniably symbolic, but of what. "What's in there?"

The man on the hill shrugged. He noted for the first time they were dressed alike, long linen shirt over dark gray breeches, the same clothes he'd worn to the bedchamber when he'd—

"Enough!" he nearly yelled at him. "It's bad enough I have to know about it. I don't want to see it in your mind as well."

"Geraint," he murmured softly, "you are aware we are the same person."

Now, it was his turn to cross his arms, reminding him of a petulant child. Was he really this bad back then? "What sort of sorcery allows a man to live for so long? What sort of spell did she put on me?"

"Enid? You blame Enid? This was none of her doing."

And then he stared at him pointedly and felt a dread pass through him. Yes, he did have a determination back then that the erosion of time had buried somewhat. "I know she enchanted me, perhaps a spell."

"No friend, that was just lust, then love, of course, an enchantment surely, but not of her making. Enid has done her best to protect you."

"Protect me? From what?"

And then Ethan's eyes fell on the dark forest, and he understood. The leaves rustled, and then the branches gave way as the great gray wolf pushed through the tangled vines and bounded toward them until he stood between Geraint and himself. The former Arthurian knight's eyes widened with surprise but not exactly fear.

"He is familiar," he whispered as he hesitantly reached out to touch the glistening fur of the imposing beast.

"Yes, he is part of us. We are all one, Brother."

Staring at the wolf, then Geraint looked up at Ethan with alarm. "She's gone," he whispered roughly.

♦

Ethan opened his eyes in the bedchamber. Sitting up, he noted that the place in the bed beside him was indeed empty. The wall tapestries hanging over the window had the faintest light of an early dawn creeping through at their edges. He sat up, trying to feel.

"*I'm sorry,*" he heard Aneira's voice in his mind.

"Why, what's happened?"

"*She was too strong. She's broken through my enchantment.*"

♦

Once she had obtained a horse from the stable, not her usual mare, she threw a heavy gray woolen cloak over her dress. In this, she would not be easily recognized as she headed directly toward the outskirts of the village.

Enid's heart was beating frantically. The voice she continued to hear in her mind she had identified as clearly Bethel's. She'd pushed down the fears that had arisen when she recognized the healer's cries in her mind. She needed her now. Bethel would help her sort out what had happened because she knew without question that the man she'd left behind in her bed was not her husband Geraint, nor was he a stranger to her.

Enid took a path circumventing the heart of the village and skirting it until she reached the lonely little cottage. The old woman had requested she be apart from the other villagers and have just enough land to plot a small garden for her herbs and vegetables. Enid felt sorry for her but also desperately needed her aid. With her help, she had contained Geraint's transformations during the lunar cycles. Bethel had told her that she could not cure him. But what she hadn't explained was the strain that this would cause. During other times, he'd become more combative and restless, just disappearing for long stretches wandering, making Enid incredibly anxious. And, the truth was that since his illness he seemed less in love with his young wife. Her very presence seemed to vex him at times.

She'd questioned Bethel about this. And the old woman just looked at her coldly and replied, "Would you rather he scourge the countryside as a monster? It is your choice, my dear."

And then there were the other ones to consider — the dark ones who had taken her husband from her and brought this madness down upon their house. They wanted him very much to join them. And if that happened, she would lose him forever.

She tied off the horse at the back of Bethel's cottage and quickly knocked on her door. Having no answer, "Bethel," she called. "Bethel, it is Enid." But still, there was nothing. The silence chilled her. She tried the latch on the door and found it gave easily. In fact, too easily, as she took in the splinters of broken wood along the edges of the entrance.

The cottage's interior was shadowed and cold as she nervously noticed immediately no fire lit. So odd. That wasn't like Bethel. The old woman constantly complained about the aches of her limbs and always kept it warm inside.

"Bethel," she called out again, nearly whispering but feeling her dread mounting. Perhaps she should leave and go home. Geraint would not be happy not to find her next to him. Last night had been so lovely, again like the earliest days of their marriage when she felt certain and secure in his regard.

And then, she noted the open door to the only other room in the cottage. Surely, if Bethel was in there, she would have heard her calling her name. Unless, unless she was in a very deep sleep. She had willfully shut down her fears of the old woman's fate as imagination. But now they resurfaced. Enid thought to leave, but something was pulling her, something unsettling she felt everywhere.

"*No, Enid,*" the barest tendril of a whisper. Was it the Fairy of the Wildwood returned to her after all this time? She'd been absent, absent when she needed her. "*I am here.*"

But she pushed it aside. Enid knew she must take control of her life, or she would always be weak and just subject to the whims of others. She took several quick steps into the bedroom and saw the bed. Bethel was indeed there, lying within it under her quilted blankets. But she was not sleeping. Her eyes were open, wide open, staring forward in horror.

An unrelenting coldness washed over Enid as she moved toward her. Without thought, almost compelled, she reached out to touch the old woman's face. A shiver ran through her as she realized the skin was as ice.

Dizziness passed through her as well as nausea, but then, in the next instant, Bethel's bony hand darted from beneath the covers, grasping her arm painfully. The eyes fixed on her, and the old woman screeched in a horrible croak, "Your husband has killed me."

Enid wrenched free in terror, yanking herself backward. But then there was silence, and Bethel again was motionless in the bed, just as Enid had first found her. Panic overtook her as she stumbled aimlessly backward into the main room of the cottage. Enid spun around, determined to flee this place of death, but found jarringly in that moment that she was not alone.

Sitting down at Bethel's small table in her darkened kitchen was a man, if she could call him that, dressed imposingly in silver and black, the one from the wolf clan that wanted Geraint for their own.

Lapetus eyed her calmly, even curiously. "Lady Enid, I understand you might be having some difficulty. Perhaps I can help."

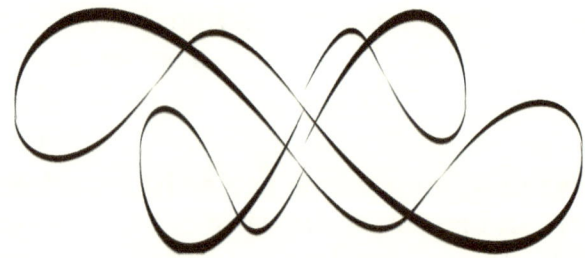

# Chapter 25

# UNWRITTEN

D isorientation and dizziness swept through him simultaneously. For a moment, Ethan thought he was back at his
home in New Orleans. But then everything shifted, and
his awareness returned to the cold bedchamber in his father's
house. "What's happening?" he whispered as he became cognizant that he was unclothed beneath the blankets.

*"You can't stay here forever. As you can see, Geraint is already
stirring in the slumber he was placed in. He's powerful as is your wife
in all her incarnations,"* again Aneira's disembodied voice.

He rubbed his temples to dispel a pervasive headache. "You
said Enid broke free of your enchantment."

*"Yes, Etienne, more quickly than I expected. Then again, the two
of you in your intimacy gave her energy, enough energy to restore
herself."*

He nodded. Yes, that had always been the way with them, as
it was with Erin now. "Erin?" he asked.

*"She's all right. Focus, Etienne, I fear your wife is coming to the realization of who she is dealing with now."*

"How could she?"

*"It seems she has new counsel."*

♦

"Why are you here?" Enid said shakily. And then a treacherous thought crossed her mind. "Did you kill Bethel?"

"That old hag? I wouldn't expend the effort," Lapetus replied with evident disdain.

She crossed her arms in front of her protectively. She was vulnerable, so much more vulnerable than the last time they'd met. "Well, someone did. She was murdered."

His silvery eyes locked on to her coldly. "And do you know who that someone is, my Lady?"

"Of course not, she was dead when I arrived," she answered with no conviction.

"Ah, too late to name her killer," he said casually, palming an apple he'd picked up from a bowl on Bethel's table. "Did I ever explain to you, my dear, the ramifications of the enchantment you used to help your husband? You know, the one where you pulled some of the demon lifeforce into yourself."

Enid took a step back. She knew she shouldn't have, but she couldn't help it. This creature, Lapetus, something about him frightened her so. "Why do you call the wolf a demon?"

He smiled. "Demon has to do with power, my Lady. We have cultivated the spirit of the dark wolf, well, for much longer than you can imagine. It is the spirit of our tribe, a collective bound together by this power. But you, you pulled a portion of that power away from your husband, undoing what it has taken us so long to build."

"I didn't want his mind corrupted," she muttered.

"Corrupted? That's a harsh word, my Lady. But in doing so, you have entangled yourself further not only with him but with us. To be exact, you owe us."

She stared at him blankly for a moment, and strangely enough, her courage returned. "That's madness. You try to take Geraint from me and say now that I owe you something."

And then he frowned, evidently not the response he desired. Lapetus stood up, straightening his long, dark cloak. "Foolish girl to make such enemies." He turned with not even a glance back at her, crossing deliberately to the doorway. His back was to her as he spoke while pausing at the entrance. "The old crone's spirit told you correctly. Your husband murdered her. What exactly does that leave you with, my Lady?" And then he left.

Enid felt a dizziness pass through her. She grasped a chair to stop herself from falling to the floor on her knees. Why, why would Geraint do such a thing to her?

◆

He dressed quickly, almost in a panic. Coming here was doing nothing except making things more complicated. It crossed his mind to try to return to his own time and let events play out in the past as they would.

*"That could be calamitous,"* whispered Aneira.

"Worse than things are now?" he responded gruffly, oddly reminding him of his former self, Geraint, who he had left on that grassy hill not long ago.

*"Yes, my Lord, believe me when I say that it could get much worse. Imagine if the dark clan gains control of Enid's power, how that poison would seep not only here but into your future. You must find a way to reach her, Etienne. She is poised on the brink of disaster."*

170

"Disaster that I have brought her to."

*"Every spirit chooses their path before birth, Etienne. You are not that omnipotent. The path of learning is chosen, but the choices we make within that path are unwritten."*

The word stabbed at him, unwritten? And now he was here to write upon Geraint and Enid's path.

*"She has returned,"* Aneira whispered.

Ethan's eyes flew to the chamber door, which was suddenly pushed open. Enid stood on the threshold quietly for a moment, her hair in disarray and a cloak loosely draped on her shoulders over her burgundy dress. He remembered now how she had always gravitated to the varying shades of the color red and how it set off her honey-blond hair.

For an instant, her expression was unreadable as her dark amber eyes cascaded over him. Then, her face animated into an abrupt smile as she walked forward, a smile that he noted did not quite reach those eyes. "My Lord, forgive me. I hoped to return before you awoke."

She threw herself into his arms, and with confusion, he cautiously wrapped his around her, returning the embrace. "Where have you been, Enid?" he murmured into her hair.

"I wanted to be outside. I walked in the sun and gathered wildflowers."

"Then all is well with you, my wife?" he asked quietly.

She tilted her head back, gazing at him lovingly, "Yes, my Lord, all is well."

And then she laid her head against his chest. And in his mind, Ethan heard Aneira's voice. *"She lies. She knows about Bethel and that you killed her."*

A coldness swept through him as he softly stroked Enid's hair. So, now they would play this game.

171

◆

When Enid was finally able to leave Bethel's cottage, she stumbled on legs that felt unstable. The confrontation with Lapetus had taken something out of her, almost as though he'd sucked the breath out of her chest.

Her head was spinning. It was too much, too much to take in, and she was alone, so very alone now. She stood outside the small dwelling, softly stroking the gray mare she'd taken from her husband's stables not so long ago.

And that was the crux of it as well. The horse, the castle, the stables, the clothes she wore all belonged to Geraint. In truth, she belonged to Geraint as well, a possession of a man who had murdered her friend.

It tore at her heart. Bethel had helped. Bethel had kept the wolf at bay. And now, what would happen at the next lunar cycle? Would Geraint transform? Would he become a monster and join the dark ones? Would he murder her in her bed as he had done with Bethel?

She stopped, her stomach clutching in nausea. As she turned her head, she uncontrollably vomited until all she could do was crouch down in weakness. How had this happened? How had everything turned so badly?

*"Enid,"* a whisper on the breeze.

She knew who it was, of course, the Fairy of the Wildwood, but she pushed her away.

"No," she muttered hotly, "you abandoned me. You foresaw this darkness in my future, and you allowed it to happen."

*"No, beloved. No one can interfere with the path of the spirit. But you must be careful, dear one. You must not act rashly, or you could cause great peril."*

"Stop it." She cried out. "If I am alone, then I will decide now what is to come." She willfully barred the Fairy from her mind, putting up intense internal barriers that Bethel had shown her not so very long ago.

"Imagine a great door made of the most impenetrable substance, my Lady. Then close it, sealing your mind from interference, and bind it with great iron locks. And know that no one will enter unless you give them leave."

Enid took this moment, closing her eyes and visualizing this great door. If nothing else was hers, then at least this would be. She took an inward breath, calming herself. With deliberation, she straightened her clothes, wiped her face, and smoothed her hair — finding herself anchored in the midst of the storm.

As she began to prepare for the journey back, a curious thought floated across her mind. She could see the woman, the one with the ginger hair she'd known in her dreams. The girl was so far away now, oddly barred from her touch. But she focused intently, finding that slowly and with much effort, she could pull her more closely.

Enid felt a coldness wrap around her heart in her resolve. Perhaps this one might be of some use to her before things were done. She pulled herself up onto the saddle of the mare and considered things, considered things carefully as she made her way back.

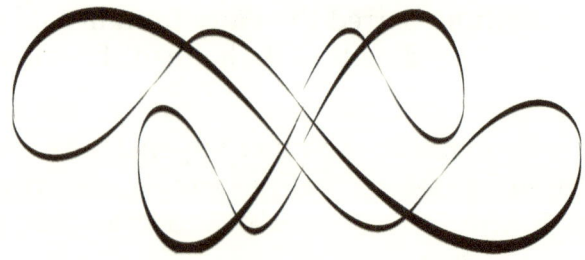

# Chapter 26

# ENCHANTMENTS

"Erin," she'd stirred in her dream. She'd been lying on the banks of a stream with her legs dangling down into the water. It was peaceful. All around her was lush forest, and the sun gently beat on her arms and her legs — not harsh but soothing and warming.

"This is my place, not yours."

She leaned back on her hands, unwilling yet to be disturbed, her face tilted to the warmth she felt.

"Did you not hear me?"

"Perhaps," Erin murmured, then lay backward on the banks of the stream. It was so soothing that she didn't want to be disrupted.

"I see. He has enchanted you."

"Ethan," Erin murmured instinctively. She could still sense his presence wrapping around her. He'd told her to rest.

"Who is Ethan?" The voice prodded abrasively. Something was wrong with it. It felt like fear.

Erin focused on the blue sky overhead, not a cloud in sight. "He is the one I love."

"Is he?" The voice said shakily. Erin felt something acutely like a tug at her, but somehow, it couldn't quite reach her.

She closed her eyes again, allowing sleepiness to overtake her, forgetting whatever or whoever was trying to reach her.

♦

Enid sat back on her legs. She was only clothed in her chemise. The candle that she'd placed within her circle burned erratically. She was in a solar room at the top of the castle. Bethel had instructed her in these ceremonies. And this was where she would cast the spells that prevented Geraint's transformation.

But the man in her bed was not Geraint, not the Geraint she recognized, and somehow, he had blocked her from pulling strength from the red-haired one. He had blocked her ability to reach her.

She bent her head, feeling taken over by a panic. What was happening? Ethan, the girl, had mentioned the name Ethan. There was a power in names. Perhaps she could use this.

She bent her head and wept. So lost, even the Fairy of the Wildwood had abandoned her. *"No, Enid,"* it whispered.

But she pushed her away. She couldn't trust her, couldn't trust anyone. This "Ethan," if he was the changeling who had taken her husband's place, then what was his goal? Would he kill her outright as he'd done with Bethel?

She sat back and concentrated on the fluttering candle. She must see. She must understand. She cleared her thoughts away, and this time focused on the man downstairs. In her mind, she could see him distinctly asleep in their bedchamber. She breathed in deeply, allowing the tendrils of her being to reach out.

She could feel power — strong power around him, skilled enchantment. Enid burrowed in and visualized more deeply, this time solely on Geraint. Her inner eyes narrowed, and she felt the pull to her husband.

Then, almost with a snap, she pulled back. Geraint was here, within the body of the man, and he was elsewhere, nearer the girl. There were so many layers of magic. She didn't understand. The only clear thing was that her husband slumbered.

A rush of fatigue passed over her. It was always this way when she attempted the spells. So much light was needed and lost.

*"Enid, you should rest and let go, dearest,"* once more the voice of the Fairy, but she swept it aside. She would not stop.

Again, she focused, holding her palms up and outward for balance. This time she concentrated on something else, on the wolf, and she felt it stirring in recognition of her. She smiled. Yes, he knew her. She had calmed and soothed him in the past.

"Guide me to the truth," she whispered.

And she found herself somewhere else, walking in a great cavern by the water.

◆

"Brother, your wife travels. You must follow her."

Ethan opened his eyes in response to Brother Guidrade's voice. There was a distinct pain in his chest as he sat up in the bed. "What's happened?" he whispered.

*"Enid is traveling, Etienne."* Aneira's voice.

He rubbed his eyes. He felt weak, almost dizzy. "What do you mean?"

*"She follows the path of the wolf. You must find her."*

He took a deep breath, feeling only disorientation, a sharp pain passing through his chest, which he placed his hand upon, his bare chest. "I feel weak," he murmured.

*"She's managed to drain you. I will help you. Just focus on Enid."*

♦

The cave floor was cold and abrasive on her bare feet. In fact, everything felt chilled as she stumbled through the vast interior. "Where am I?" she whispered, moving forward reluctantly. And then she felt something against her side, nuzzling against her leg. Looking down, she saw the great gray wolf staring up at her with his bluish eyes.

She took a quick breath but was not afraid, although he was of such a size that he could so easily rip her to pieces if that were his intent. But instead, she reached down softly, stroking his head and behind his ear. So many times in her dreams, she had seen this wolf, so to her, it was as if they were more than well-acquainted.

"Why are we here?" she whispered.

And the creature pulled away from her, simply moving forward across the great cavern. Although her feet ached, and she trembled from the cold, Enid followed him.

♦

The voice reached out from somewhere deep in her dreams. "Lady," it whispered, but strong, deep, not the feminine voice from before.

Erin opened her eyes. Above her, the bright blue sky still stretched overhead, but immediately, she knew she was not alone.

She sat up and turned, taking in the man standing some yards away. He simply stood there, looking at her with no expres-

177

sion. He was dressed in silver and black robes, so odd, she thought. But then she looked down at her garb, a long, floor-length, rose-colored dress cinched at the waist with an ornate silver belt. "What is this?" she murmured, still feeling that dreamlike quality overtaking everything.

"Green would have served you better."

Erin looked back to the dark-haired man addressing her. She momentarily stared at him in confusion, and then he shrugged a bit. Casually, he strolled over to her side, sitting cross-legged down next to her on the banks of the stream. He glanced down at her bare legs and feet submerged in the rushing water. "Isn't that cold?"

Erin considered for the first time, given that she had a visitor, that modesty might be in order, but then again, a pair of blue jean cut-off shorts she had back home in Arkansas exposed much more of her than hiking up her long skirt did now. "Not really, it's comfortable."

He nodded, saying nothing else.

"Why are you here?"

Again, a slight shrug, "Here? Yes, where is here, exactly?"

"Oh," she murmured with distraction. "I think it must be a dream."

"Ah," he said softly. "But whose dream is the question."

She gazed forward, feeling strange and disconnected again, as though she only wanted to lie back down and sleep.

"That's the spell."

"Spell? That's not possible," she responded quickly.

And then he smiled. It wasn't a warm smile like Ethan's but a little cold or even sarcastic. Erin remembered how she really detested sarcastic people. While she was blind, she could hear it so clearly in their voices, as though they were belittling everyone and everything around them.

"Sorry, I've forgotten this version of you has modern sensibilities. What we called spells, enchantments, you call energy, psychic abilities — a rose by any other name."

She frowned with irritation. There was no doubt now his presence was chafing her. "I don't think you should be here," she said cuttingly. It wasn't a demeanor she used often, but it did come in handy in the proper situations.

But this man, all it did was seem to amuse him. He glanced at her again and said softly, "As I mentioned, green would have been a better choice." Then she glanced down at her dress and understood.

"I like this one," she murmured.

"Yes, but for those on the outside, the rose color conflicts with your lovely auburn hair. Green like the primeval forest would suit you more."

"You should leave," she said again, feeling genuinely unnerved.

He leaned back on his hands as though trying to make himself comfortable. "You know, in a roundabout way, we are kindred, my Lady."

"Kindred? You mean related?"

"Yes, it seems the woman you seem linked to, the Lady Enid, took some of our power into her to save her beloved or your beloved. It's not easy to keep track of all of this."

Erin squinted her eyes a bit. So odd. It was the sun now bothering her. It hadn't before. Why would it now? It must be him, this man. Why wouldn't he just go and leave her in peace? "Power? What does that mean?"

"Oh yes, sorry, it slipped my mind, modern sensibilities. By power, I mean energy, the energy one gains from the wolf clan when they are initiated. Enid took it into herself."

"But why? Why would she?"

Again, he shrugged, "I'm not sure. To give Geraint his autonomy, I suppose. He was given a gift from the dark wolf, eternal life, and so he owes his servitude."

"Owes?"

"Indeed, but his lovely wife muddied the waters, so to speak. But she did bind herself to us and the wolf as well."

Erin stared out at the soothing, rushing water in front of her, trying to clear her mind. "What does that have to do with me?"

"Yes, that is the question. But I think, my Lady, it is time for you to wake."

"No, no, Ethan wanted me to stay here."

"Yes, well then, he shouldn't have left you alone." And then he reached out to grab her hand, and she opened her eyes.

# Chapter 27

# THE PATH OF THE WOLF

E nid pushed her honey-blond hair behind her shoulders and steeled herself. This was a vision. She had been schooled by the Fairy of the Wildwood about these symbolic manifestations and by Bethel as well, though her approach was not the same. One counseled to absorb and receive the wisdom that was being imparted while the other to take the answers that were necessary to prevail.

At times, she'd done both. But as the instability of desperation became the guiding force of her life, she'd leaned more heavily in Bethel's direction. Whether it was the proper course or not, she'd chosen to protect her husband.

Her husband? But where he was now remained shrouded from her.

The wolf bounded away across the cave and into the entrance of the next chamber.

Enid shivered. She wished she had the long red cloak her husband had given her as a gift just after her marriage. It was made of thick wool and trimmed with black fur. But instead, she wore nothing but this plain white shift, not adorned with anything and so thin. It made her feel weak and vulnerable.

"Adornments do not make one strong, my Lady."

The voice startled her. It came from the next chamber, where the wolf had disappeared. But she felt suddenly frightened, so weak. How had this come to be? She remembered so long ago being afraid, afraid of Geraint. She could see the darkness that he brought with him.

*"Lady, Enid,"* the whisper of the Fairy. *"Child, there is naught to do but go forward."*

"I'm afraid." Her voice shook.

*"Yes, but you must find the light again."*

♦

Ethan struggled to clear his mind. "Where is Enid?" he asked.

*"Wait,"* was the answer from Aneira. *"I fear Etienne, it is too late for your help. You must stay until she returns."*

♦

Enid walked barefoot across the threshold, and what she saw within was not at all what she expected.

She was surrounded by great tall trees stretching so high that they nearly touched the sky. Gazing upward, she could clearly see that it was not blue overhead but darkened and stormy. "Where am I?" she whispered.

*"Deep within,"* was the answer on the breeze. It was not the voice of the Fairy nor anyone she knew. *"We are the spirits of the forest."*

"Yes, I can feel you all around."

*"We are here to guide you, Enid, if you will it."*

Her feet ached from walking on the twigs and brambles, but she continued. "Yes, yes, I am lost. I was following the wolf."

And then she heard a soft, muffled growl, and suddenly, he sprang in front of her from behind a cluster of trees whose trunks were so thick you could build a sweet house within. Enid smiled sadly, longing to be pure again and part of the forest.

*"Nothing is lost,"* was the whisper. Where a moment before the great wolf was standing atop a great jagged tree stump, there was now sitting a man, a young man with piercing blue eyes and thick, silvery gray hair not unlike the coat of the wolf.

"Who are you?" she asked softly.

And then he grinned as if she were nonsensical. "I am the one you follow, Enid." His voice was deep and rich, although his face was so young, not a child but years younger than her husband.

"The wolf," she murmured. "I thought you were a dark spirit like Lapetus."

"I am not good or bad," he said softly, caressing the words in nearly a growl. "But am shaded by the hearts of men."

She smiled. He wore a great gray cloak, a shade darker than his hair, again just like the variegated fur of the wolf. Why had she feared him so much? She had no idea now.

"It is time to let go, my Lady. Your husband and I will make our own pact."

Her heart sank at his proclamation, "But then what will become of me?"

And then he smiled again, baring teeth that were dazzlingly white. "Whatever you wish, my Lady. It is your choice."

"But the others—"

"Will find their own way." He finished for her.

183

She glanced around, feeling so drawn by this enchanted place. "Can I stay here, please?"

"No, angel, you are not done with your world yet. But perhaps one day." And he sprung to his feet lithely just like the wolf had and stood before her. "Now return, sweet Enid, and he moved nearer, kissing her lightly on the lips." But when she awoke, she was not in her solar room but rather in her bed within her chamber. She closed her eyes once, then opened them again to make quite sure where she was. Indeed, it was her bedchamber, but the spot beside her was vacant.

Where was he?

She glanced about, suddenly shaken, observing the light creeping through the wall tapestries at the windows. Was it moonlight? Had she forgotten the cycle of the moon? But then her heart calmed as she remembered the young man with the blue eyes — not so frightening.

Again, she peered about the great chamber. The wooden door well beyond the foot of the bed was closed. Where had he gone?

And then she heard a slight movement across the room in front of one of the tapestries covering a far window. She pulled the covers tightly up around her chemise. She still couldn't quite see through the blackness.

Finally, she heard a voice, a quiet voice. "Be still, my wife. I am here."

"Geraint," she whispered, hesitating on the name because she still did not know who he truly was. "Why are you sitting alone in the shadows?"

"Thinking, love."

And then she heard movement, and a candle was suddenly lit on the table beside him. Ghostly, his face seemed pale next to the flickering light, as though life had been drained out of it. "Are you ill, my husband?"

"That is a question. But I have been considering, watching closely, and weighing matters profoundly these last few days."

Enid took a sharp breath. *"Calm,"* was the whisper around her.

He moved silently from across the room, bringing the candle with him and setting it quietly on the table next to her. His long linen shirt was unbuttoned, and she could see him clearly in the dim light. And then he sat beside her on the bed, taking her hand in his. "Where have you been, Enid?" he asked softly. Geraint, the one she knew, rarely spoke in such a quiet voice, only when he held her close in the darkness.

"Where?" she repeated.

He squeezed her hand, "Yes, it is time to drop the pretense. I know you have been away, elsewhere, to a place conjured perhaps by some dark magic."

"Not all magic is dark, my husband," and then she pulled her hand out of his. "If that is indeed who you are," she whispered.

She heard him sigh. "Will you believe me if I say that I am? I am Geraint, and also Etienne, and many other names I have had over many many years."

And then she looked up into his eyes, shadowed now. "Ethan?" she murmured.

"Yes, where did you—"

"The one with the red hair, she is yours."

He smiled a little sadly in a way that clawed at her heart because she did not remember seeing this disturbing expression in his eyes before. "It's complicated."

"I believe you," Enid replied. "But you are not the Geraint I know."

"No, no, I am not. But he is with me."

"Then why are you here?"

"I am here because you needed me because—" then he stopped, seeming reluctant to continue.

"You asked where I was. I traveled the wolf's path and met his spirit deep in the forest."

"His spirit?" he murmured.

She nodded slowly. "Yes, he convinced me to let you, well, Geraint and he make their own peace. I have decided to do so. I no longer have the strength to prevent it, nor do I have the fear I have carried with me."

"I see," he said softly. "That seems wise to me."

"Yes, now I ask that you answer my question, whoever you wish to be now." He straightened up and eyed her with a measure of wariness that she picked up on immediately. "I would like to know why you killed my friend."

◆

Erin opened her eyes to find herself in the bedroom at Ethan's house near the Lakefront. She looked around the room, feeling utterly disoriented, as though a languidness hung over her intensely. She stood up from the bed, trying to straighten her clothes. So strange, it felt as though she'd been in such a heavy sleep for so long. She quietly walked into the den, feeling inexplicably panicked to find Ethan. There was something, something she needed to tell him, but exactly what it was, she couldn't remember.

Immediately when she crossed into the room, she saw someone standing in front of the window that overlooked the back patio.

But then, almost immediately, her heart clutched with fear. It clearly wasn't Ethan. His hair was dark. What was a stranger doing in his house?

He turned around slowly, and Erin jarringly recognized him from her dream. It was the man who'd spoken to her, the man dressed in the cloak of silver and black. He smiled slowly in a way that greatly unnerved her. "Erin Holt, I've been waiting for you to wake up."

"Who are you?" she whispered shakily.

"My name is Lapetus."

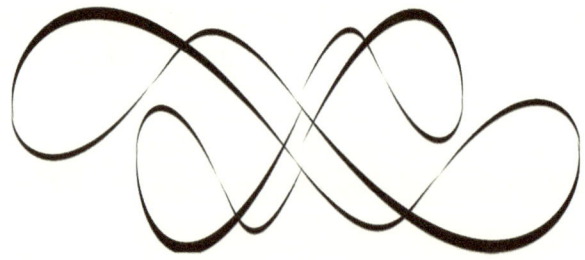

# Chapter 28

# INCARNATIONS

"*She's unique, my daughter.*"

Ethan remembered Robbert Kinglon's words as he stared into the shadowed eyes of his wife, Enid. A chill traversed his spine. Foolish man, he wondered, did he really know her at all? "What did you say," he murmured.

Stoic, cool, this was a description of her he did not remember from, well, from so long ago. Then again, maybe time and discord had blurred the truth of her in his eyes. Perhaps he'd come to idolize her, meld her into some sort of imagined image instead of who she was, the flesh and blood woman before him.

"You're not Geraint, not exactly, are you? And I do know that you killed Bethel. Even I knew that she wasn't a pure soul, but she was helpful to me. And I don't believe she deserved—"

"Deserved to have her neck snapped?" he said with no emotion.

And then, even in the dim light of the chamber, he could see her pale a bit at his bluntness. "So that's what you did to her."

"It was quick," he said with coldness. "But necessary."

"Was it?" she answered sharply. Well, he'd angered her. That might be easier to deal with than detachment. "Why, did you think you had the right?"

And then he grasped her arms, not in tenderness, but instead, deep frustration. "Because she was leading you down a dark path, Enid. She was changing who you are."

"Who I am. How do you know who I am?" She whispered indignantly.

And then his fingers bit into her arms, and he saw her wince in pain. Was all this leading only to a place where they would hurt each other? "I know you," he answered, still questioning if he'd ever really seen her or only what, in his obtuseness, he wanted to see.

"You are not my husband."

"And what would he say, Enid? If he knew how you'd been controlling him if he knew the alliances you'd been making."

And then she pulled back in a yank, abruptly breaking the contact. "What alliances do you speak of?"

"The dark witch, Bethel, and the other from the wolf clan, Lapetus."

"I've made no alliance there," she said shakily. "And I was only protecting Geraint, not trying to control—"

"You made choices for him." It felt so odd, speaking of himself in the third person. "Choices you had no right to make."

She shook her head, eyes suddenly filling with tears. Yes, good, he was reaching his wife again, not so hard, not so unfeeling as she would like him to think. "Who are you to judge? Murderer, deceiver, taking me to my husband's bed."

And then he reached out, grabbing her forcibly, "Enid, I am he. Surely you can see that. I am Geraint. Changed, hardened, eroded, molded by time, and yes, maybe for the worse in some respects, but maybe for the better in others. This curse, this affliction, has caused me to live, live on through centuries well beyond our lifetime. But I am here now because of you, to help you," and then he stopped at her expression. Her eyes were so wide, shocked, and her chin trembled, perhaps in astonishment or perhaps simply terror. There was too much emotion to sort through.

"That cannot be," she whispered hollowly.

The air seemed to leave his lungs in weariness. "My path has been long and solitary. There has been no one, truly, my wife, since you left me."

"Not no one, the one with the red hair," she murmured.

He took in a painful breath. Perhaps he'd been wrong explaining this to her.

"*She needs to know,*" Aneira's voice coaxed him.

"Her name is Erin," he said quietly.

"Erin, and who is this woman that has finally taken your heart from me?"

He stared into her darkened eyes, wondering if she was even capable of comprehending what was coming. Beginning with deliberation, "Enid, this will be difficult to understand, but she is you. She has your eternal spirit, which has reincarnated on the earth in another body."

For a moment, there was a gulf of silence between them. Perhaps she thought him mad. After all, this was medieval times. But she just continued to gaze at him, wide-eyed, as though trying to absorb what he'd said to her. Then, finally spoke softly in a voice that almost sounded defeated. "So, I battle myself for your love."

And then impulsively, he pulled her tightly into his arms because he could not help himself. And whispered to her softly, "You have always had my love, Enid."

♦

He'd held her for some time and then made love to her again in her husband's bed, but then again, if all of this was not madness, it was his bed as well. But Enid lay awake in the darkness long after she'd heard the man beside her fall asleep, wondering, pondering.

Could he be speaking the truth?

Could she truly be lying next to her husband from the future, a man somehow involved in his time with a future incarnation of herself?

She knew of the spirit from the teachings of the Fairy of the Wildwood, someone who'd professed to be the spirit of her deceased mother.

*"Flesh does not last, but the spirit is eternal,"* she'd taught her.

But Geraint, or at least the man beside her, claimed to be of the same flesh as her husband, destined to walk the earth for an endless time in the same body that did not age. Bethel had not wholly explained the curse of the wolf to her, only that he would transform into the uncontrollable beast upon the cycle of the full moon.

And he had insisted that the old woman was leading her down a dark path. For perhaps the first time, Enid considered the herbs that Bethel had concocted to prevent Geraint's transformation. They did seem to prevent it. Only two times she'd slipped them into his ale. But the morning after, it was undeniable that Geraint was sickened and so abrasive to her, not at all himself. Once, he'd even raised his hand to strike her in anger but then barely stopped himself, seeming confused as to what was occurring. There was no doubt that there were costs to Bethel's treatments. But in her fear and anxiety for Geraint, Enid had chosen to overlook them.

As she weighed these events, she reflected that Bethel had also pushed her to use more spells and even draw the life force from the woman she could see in her visions, the one with the red hair. Draining her power was how Bethel had phrased it. So, in some respect, she was damaging her future self, though it wasn't precisely her. Incarnations were complicated as had been explained by the Fairy of the Wildwood.

It all felt puzzling, although there was a ring of truth in this Ethan's words. She could not call him Geraint as he did not truly seem to be her husband, although her body responded to him as though he was.

But the man who had just lain with her had also killed Bethel. He was a ruthless man in some respects, as was Geraint when he felt it was warranted.

And Lapetus? His cold threats still rang in her ears. He had found a weakening in their defenses, and she sensed that he was poised to come after them both.

Enid closed her eyes, trying to clear her mind. It was too much, too much to absorb, too confusing. She longed for the simplicity of her life with Geraint before, before the wolf attack, when all that mattered was that they were beside one another. She breathed in deeply, allowing these concerns to float away as she focused on peace, peace within the forest.

And as she did, the voices began to float inward.

*"What are you doing here?"*

*"Waiting for you to wake, my dear."*

*"What have you done with Ethan?"*

*"Done?"* Enid could see his form solidify in her mind as he slowly spun around. Clothed in strange garments, but it was the

same face. It was Lapetus. *"I haven't done anything, Erin,"* he said slowly, as though experimenting with the texture of her name on his lips. *"He remains in some sort of deep meditation, and it would seem rude of me to try to pull him out of it. So, I decided to wait, though I couldn't help but wonder where he was traveling to."*

*"Traveling?"* The red-haired one, Erin, seemed to stumble over her words. She was afraid. Enid could feel it, feel it acutely in her skin. But, of course, she was. Enid had felt with their first contact that this one had her own sensitivities, her own gifts. She couldn't help but sense Lapetus' malevolent nature.

And then he smiled, moving more closely to her. *"Yes, traveling, my dear. His spirit is not in his body at present, though it does not seem as though he has left himself entirely unprotected. Still, you might be another matter."*

She stepped back, definitely afraid. *"What do you want?"* she said, not at all reflecting that fear. She was strong. That was good for whatever might come.

*"Want? That's a good question. I think for now I'll wait, wait for your lover to wake up, so we can all have a long overdue talk."*

# Chapter 29

# A VILLAIN

H e breathed in the cool air of the forest. This time, he was not sitting on the outside, but somewhere within, deep within, though with enough room to walk and see a gray sky stretching overhead in a foreboding way.

"Not so easy, is it, Brother, trying to find the right path."

He glanced several feet away where his likeness was leaning against a mossy-covered tree that seemed to stretch up infinitely or at least far enough to pierce that very gray sky.

"What is this place?" he murmured, looking around — not a normal forest, surely.

"No, not ordinary," Geraint said, straightening up. "Though I do remember it. I was on a quest from the Queen. She'd been insulted by a knight from some neighboring province, and I was trailing him to seek—" and then he laughed, "justice, retribution, revenge, who knows. How simple things seemed in those days. But I do remember passing through this forest. I felt as though it was filled with sorcery, magic perhaps. And when I entered it, that was when I found Enid."

"Yes, she was sitting beside a stream," Ethan replied thoughtfully.

"Asleep, I think, her legs dangling in the water. Such beautiful legs, I thought she was a nymph."

Ethan echoed his sentiments, "I remember. Magic, yes, she was always magic."

"Is she now, my friend? Your Erin, is she magic too?"

Ethan swallowed on a dry throat, feeling so many things but primarily guilt at the moment. "Yes," he said softly.

"And I wonder what you would do to protect her. I know that for Enid, I would do anything."

His eyes narrowed, staring at his conscience in living flesh conferring with him. "Yes, anything."

♦

Ethan opened his eyes in the darkened chamber and saw that the place beside him was empty. "Enid," he called, glancing around with concern, and then he found her. He could make out her form in the shadows, standing in front of a tapestry-covered window. She had pulled the heavy drape aside and was staring outside. "There is movement in the darkness. They are coming for us," she murmured.

He quickly moved from the bed, crossing to her. "What do you see?"

"Nothing," she whispered. "It is what I feel in my skin. Like you, I am connected to the wolf clan."

He softly put his hands on her shoulders. "Tell me."

"Lapetus and some others of his clan will lay siege to your castle if you do not come to them."

"How do you know this?"

"He has told me," she replied with no emotion. "We must settle this."

"Yes, I know," he answered gravely.

"No, you must go back soon. Your Erin is in danger now. Time has run out."

◆

*A Villain*

*What constitutes a villain? It is an ancient question that the great philosophers contemplated, often, repeatedly, and with no consistent conclusions. It is a question I have turned over in my mind occasionally as well. Thus, in my vast experience and within the scope of my long, protracted lifetime, I have concluded that defining a villain seems to lie largely in perspective. Outside of extreme examples, mass murderers, horrific despots, and the like, most villains don't usually see themselves in that regard.*

*As a prime example, I offer myself. I have been hunted in my lifetime, termed a beast, and, yes, have killed, some might say, unjustly. So, am I the villain? Well, it's my tale, my chronicle, though I try to be even-handed and fair in its retelling, though unequivocally, I would have to say not.*

*But Lapetus, my pseudo adopted Brother, might he be a villain?*

*He certainly dresses the part, seems sinister enough, and does try to impose his will. But does he believe so?*

*Probably not, no, probably not at all.*

◆

"Balor has returned. He says there is no stirring from the castle. Perhaps Geraint will not meet this challenge."

"He will," he whispered more confidently than he felt. Earlier in the evening, he'd sent the message through the connection he'd forged with the woman, Enid. Lapetus felt restless to end the threat he felt from the Cymry Prince. It must be settled. Either he, though now they, must join the clan, or they both die. There would be no middle ground.

*"Must it always be so?"* a whisper on the wind. Lapetus turned around, staring toward the forest that began at the bottom of the hill below him. His eyes were accustomed to visions, but at this moment, he saw nothing, not even a wavering of the trees.

"This place is cursed," Kian whispered hotly. "We should abandon this and return home."

"Without Geraint?" murmured Lapetus. "His blood could strengthen our clan."

"Or usurp your authority. Do you really believe he would ever allow himself to be led by anyone?"

"He was led by his King."

"That is a unique matter, far afield—" Then he stopped, evidently not wanting to continue.

"But how could I let them go? It would encourage others to follow his lead," Lapetus replied, though almost to himself.

His eyes remained on the trees as he truly felt the anticipation of something, and suddenly, now through the darkness, he could see movement, shadows fluttering. Something was there, deep within, waiting for him. "We follow out of loyalty, my Lord, not fear."

"Maybe," he whispered with distraction. "Maybe some do." And then, as in response, a figure stepped out, separating from the darkness. Lapetus caught his breath. He remembered he'd been told this forest bordered worlds, and spirits walked within. "Kian, go check on the others. Wait for me with them."

"Yes, my liege," he said hesitantly. Lapetus waited until he could no longer hear Kian's footfalls, then began the short de-

197

scent down the hill. Just as he approached, the slim, shadowed figure turned and headed back into the dense woods. So, it was clear now that he would have to follow. He took a deep breath and steeled himself just before he entered.

*"Why have you chosen me?"*

The trees were ominous, even to someone like him who traveled through the shadows.

*"I cannot lead."* Whispers from his past, when he was a younger man just recently indoctrinated.

*"It is done."* Had been the answer to everything, no choice.

There never was a choice. The clan moved as one mind, one thought, which was survival. *"What is our purpose?"*

*"To perpetuate."* It was the only response he ever received.

Lapetus continued to follow despite twigs, branches, and other indefinable tugging at his clothing. The scratches he ignored as inconsequential and easily healed, a side effect of being one with the wolf. But Lapetus traveled forward, un-daunted, tracking, as was his natural instinct, until he found himself in a clearing only illuminated by the light of a crescent moon. The figure had stopped but remained with his back to him.

"What do you require of me?" he asked solemnly.

And then it turned, a slight form, a very young man. The face was angular and well-sculpted but youthful. But it was the eyes that haunted. They were silvery, pure, and only silver, unearthly, reflecting at him in a face that seemed like a mask in this setting. Even for him, it was a jolt. He'd had visions of the wolf spirit many times over the course of his long existence, but never quite like this.

"Why?" it whispered, nearly in a growl.

"Why what?" he stumbled over the question.

"Why do you seek the blood of your Brother?"

"I-" he stopped, jolted. "It is our law. All must be part of the clan, as it has always been."

The wolf spirit pulled back his hood. His hair was black, thick, just like his. That was as he would always see it in dreams, a great black majestic wolf. But this child before him. It felt oddly vulnerable, unnatural. Perhaps it was this place, so far from the land they called home. And then it smiled, animating the expressionless features. "You expected a monster?"

"No," Lapetus answered, nearly choking on the lie. "I expected power."

"And I do not represent power to you?" The boy-man laughed softly. "Again, why do you seek to harm your Brother?"

"If he is not one with us, he is a threat."

The spirit tilted its head again as though somehow Lapetus amused him. "You have served us well, Lapetus. But the old ways will not always suffice. There may yet be a use for the renegade wolf and his mate. Do not be so dogmatic that you cannot see our future."

Lapetus opened his eyes, unaware that they'd been closed. Again, he stood on the hill near the edge of the dark forest, firmly footed as though he had never left here. His head swam with the scent of the abundant trees in his nostrils. Had he been there with the wolf spirit, or had it been some sort of vision?

On the side of the grassy hill, he could see Kian quickly ascending with Balor and Cael. "My Lord, Geraint is approaching."

"Is he alone?" he asked.

"No, his Lady rides with him."

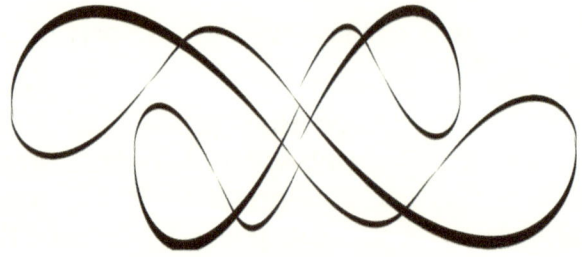

# Chapter 30

# STRATEGIZING

L apetus stared out the patio window overlooking a small courtyard and stone fountain in Ethan Garraint's yard. Evidently, his Brother had steeped himself in the culture of the area. Kian seemed quite taken with the city as well, but for himself, he grew restless, so far away from his home across the ocean. He'd never adapted well to traveling, although from time to time, necessity dictated it.

He briefly glanced over to the woman sitting nervously on the sofa. Her eyes were locked on the doorway, waiting tentatively for her paramour to appear and ostensibly rescue her from him. He coolly returned his gaze to the outside. So odd, his senses continued to feel something familiar from her, an awareness that he'd always connected to Geraint's bride, Enid.

But that tendril that stirred recognition was fleeting. What indeed was the link, the secret between them? These women couldn't be more different, though Enid herself had evolved over time. He remembered that fateful night when they initiated her husband into the wolf clan. Of course, for them, the outsiders, it had seemed like a vicious attack. Little did they know that Geraint had been carefully tracked and chosen to become a Brother, as had always been their way. But Enid, so weak, so helpless, so overcome with grief with her husband's bloodied and dying body in her arms — how she wept.

He supposed he could have killed her. The female line rarely, even back then, made the transformation into the wolf clan, only particular ones who were unique.

And if he'd killed her then, it might have been easier for the clan to claim Geraint as their own. If only—

But the truth was that something about her stirred pity within him. It was a deep pity, a surprising one, that with the inordinate passage of time and harsh events, he'd felt certain had been exorcised from him. With some distraction, he watched a few passing blue jays lightly landing on the stone fountain at the center of the yard. Of course, they were a sign. What had his mother told him from such a long time ago, so many lifetimes ago? She was a healer and would often read the omens sent by nature.

*"The blue ones are a sign of transition, my child. Do not resist the change."*

"He's left you unprotected for some time. I wonder that he's not worried for your safety," he murmured aloud.

"Are you threatening me?" She asked coldly in a very measured voice. Well, maybe this one was not as vulnerable as he'd previously thought.

He smiled, oddly reminded again of Lady Enid. "Just an observation. Threats can appear in all sorts of unexpected places."

She didn't answer him, just as well. He could, of course, just leave, leave them alone to whatever this was. Or he could kill her, Geraint's new Lady love, as he should have done to his wife so long ago. But what would that achieve, except some solace born of a need to tidy up loose ends? And as a consequence, it would spur a vendetta on the part of her lover. So why was he here? Good question.

He took a deep breath and allowed his mind to turn backward to that fateful night from the distant past. He recalled them, Enid and Geraint riding toward them on a great pale horse. She wore a long cloak, a shade of forest green, and her husband was dressed in black. He laughed softly, clothed not unlike the Grim Reaper. Perhaps that was his intent to be the bringer of death, perhaps. But that was not how things unfolded.

◆

"They will not expect you as you are," she whispered in his ear as they traveled through the darkness.

"What does that mean?" Ethan asked, feeling Enid's arms wrapped tightly around him as they traveled on his stallion together. There had been a bit of an argument before they'd even gotten this far.

◆

"It's not safe. You must stay."

Her face had blanched quite visibly at his pronouncement. "I was the one who told you of their approach. I need to be there."

"Why?" he asked with suspicion. So much had happened, had occurred between them that he couldn't help but wonder if he could really trust his wife anymore.

And then she stopped, almost as though frozen. "I see," she whispered.

He pulled on Geraint's heavy black cloak made of wool and trimmed with brown fur. It had always been one of his favorites. "See? What exactly?"

"You think I am in league with them, with Lapetus."

He hesitated, "Well, although I doubt that is true, I am not comfortable with the amount of time you've spent in his company as of late."

She drew in a sharp breath, "Yes, that is true. It was misguided, I admit. So, allow me to make amends. Let me help you."

He eyed her with concern. "And you're so sure that you can do so?"

"I know you believe otherwise. But my time with Bethel was not wasted. I have learned ways, spells, incantations that might cause distraction. You will be outnumbered, my husband."

He noted that when she said the words "my husband," her voice did seem to falter. It was clear that Enid believed his story but still did not fully equate him with the man she'd married. "Perhaps, but the moon isn't full, and it is my hope that this will impede their transformation."

"Yes, but yours—" she whispered.

"Is a different matter," he said quietly.

"Let me come with you, Ethan," she said his name carefully as though it was truly problematic for her to speak.

*"Etienne, relent,"* the softest whisper of Aneira in support of her daughter.

◆

They'd opted to ride on one horse, his horse, the faithful Uasail, who had seemed to accept him wholeheartedly even after all these years.

"What will they expect?" he asked Enid.

"I cannot be certain, but I believe that Lapetus is privy to the fact that Geraint has never fully changed into the wolf. He will expect you to be more vulnerable than you are. It is an advantage that you should not relinquish too quickly."

He smiled at her cleverness, "And when did you become such a strategist, Enid?"

She laughed softly, "I always was. You just did not notice, my Lord."

His heart was saddened at that. It did seem as though there was much that had escaped him about his lovely young wife. Pity that he had missed so much in his obtuseness when he was with her.

"And how will they expect me to approach them?"

She hesitated, but he felt her hands grip him more tightly as they rode. "Angry and protective."

"Protective? Truly? Then, why would you be with me?"

And then he heard her sigh softly, "Perhaps because Geraint might believe I betrayed him. He or you, rather if you remember, was very possessive and jealous."

"Yes, that I do remember."

♦

It was quite puzzling as he saw them approach. Lapetus and his men waited on that very hill that descended to the forest. He'd only brought a few to support him, Kian, Balor, and Taranis. Even without the transformation to the wolf, the members of the clan were quite formidable, strong as they'd lived under the power of the wolf clan's blood for hundreds of years already.

A new initiate would not yet benefit or obtain that strength quickly. And one who had not fully accepted the evolution, as Geraint had not, would be weaker yet.

This was what he knew. But as the two approached, husband and wife, he sensed something different — smelled it rather with his acute senses. Lapetus couldn't understand it, but he smelled power.

Just short of the foot of the grassy hill, Geraint stilled his horse. Lithely, he swung off its back and then lifted his Lady to the ground. "Why have you brought Enid, my Brother? This is none of her concern." Lapetus asked with steel in his voice.

"I am not sure that is so, as it was she that you contacted rather than I."

He nodded. He suspected his wife. Well, just as well. She had been plotting behind his back for some time. "I do not seek violence, Geraint, just understanding and compliance."

"What sort of compliance?" he asked. Lapetus noted the woman just stood beside him, somewhat timidly, he thought. Yet something about even that struck a discordant note in him.

Lapetus began to move toward him, but Kian put a hand on his shoulder. "My Brother, something is amiss. Do not put yourself in harm's way."

"It's all right, Kian," he murmured under his breath. "They are weak."

"That is not what I sense," he whispered. "The woman is a witch."

His eyes narrowed. Was this true? Had she benefitted from that old hag that her husband had lately murdered? "Are we going to negotiate, Lapetus? Or would you rather continue to scramble with your followers?"

A flash of anger darted across his spine. He was arrogant. What cause allowed him to be so arrogant? "They are not followers, Geraint. They are my Brothers, as are you."

Even in the darkness, he could see Geraint's eyes tracking him relentlessly. And the woman, Enid, whispered silently to herself. Perhaps a prayer, perhaps something else.

"You mistake yourself. An attack and a bite of poison does not make us Brothers."

"Geraint, you do not understand the full import of what has been given you. Your bride has stolen that from you."

"Enough," Geraint nearly roared in his direction. "I want you gone, all of you, from my lands. I want never to see your face again, Brother, for the rest of my days." He nearly spat out at him with venom in his voice.

"The rest of your days, that could be somewhat longer than you imagine," Lapetus hissed in response.

"This is my will, and you will abide by it."

"Abide by it, Geraint? And how do you expect to enforce your will against us?"

And in that instant — was it an instant — because it oddly felt to Lapetus as though time had stopped. It was as though some fog, some mist, had wrapped about him and captured and frozen his thoughts for just a moment. And when, with sheer will, he was able to finally shatter and break free of this confusion, he found that Geraint was no longer at the bottom of the hill but standing in front of him with his hand wrapped around his neck.

"What enchantment is this?" Lapetus rasped through the crushing grip as he saw the fingernails on Geraint's hands begin to grow into the claws of the wolf.

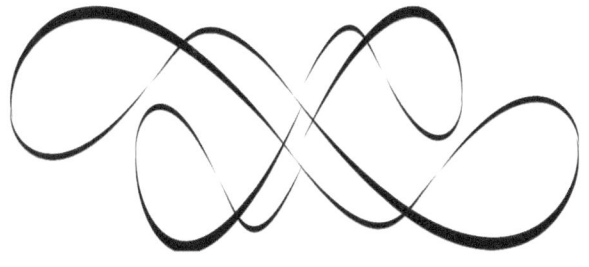

# Chapter 31

# FOR THE LAST TIME

As Ethan felt his fangs grow, the ancient stirring of the beast led him forward. The control he'd learned to exact over the centuries seemed to melt away as he was caught up in the instinctual blood lust. All he could desire was to taste flesh and sink his teeth cruelly and without mercy into Lapetus' throat. But in the flicker of an instant, everything shifted as though a great quake of some kind jarred him out of his present, dragging him into another place.

◆

His mind swirled with disorientation, and for a moment, he considered that he could be returning to his own time. But when everything solidified, it became clear that this was not the case. Ethan found himself on his knees, his face down, nearly planted on the grassy, lush bed of a dense forest. As he painfully turned his head, he saw not many yards away from him, Lapetus also in the same prone position.

"Not a very pleasant way for Brothers to treat each other." The voice was masculine but light and young in his ears, though also resounding powerfully through his mind. Ethan sat backward on his legs, breathing deeply, and what he saw was perched on a nearby tree trunk that had evidently fallen in the forest but was still tangled with growing vines and blooming wildflowers.

"What are you, some Fairy creature?" he whispered raggedly to the young man settled atop the trunk with his legs crossed. Undeniably, even with everything he had witnessed during his very long tenure on this Earth, this was an odd-looking being, elf-like in some respects, with angular features and eyebrows that darted upward quite dramatically. The youth wore a hood that he now reached up to slowly draw down to his shoulders. And it struck him with surprise. Though obviously young, this boy possessed a full head of gray hair, lush, full, but gray, nonetheless. And he smiled back at Ethan with a broad smile and silvery-blue eyes that almost bent up in a crescent shape, just like a —

"Moon," Lapetus said plainly in response to Ethan's observations. "Mind your thoughts here," he grumbled. "They're as loud as the spoken word."

Slowly, Ethan began to move to rise from his knees, but the pixyish man cautioned him. "Stay as you are. I want no more threatening actions from you."

In response, and with a frown, Lapetus also sat backward on his legs in a similar position. "How could you control the wolf's transformation? We are only beginning to master this. It has taken us hundreds of years," he snapped at Ethan.

"No, Lapetus, we are here for another purpose," the youth scolded him.

In response, his nemesis' eyes returned to the young man before them. "As you wish, my liege."

"My liege?" Ethan questioned. "You know this boy?"

"Tell him." The youth commanded with little inflection in his voice.

"This, he, is the spirit of the wolf clan, of the wolf."

Ethan looked to him blankly, disbelieving momentarily, and then another thought intruded. His hair, the gray — he had seen the wolf in visions, dreams, and it was always that rich, varied shade of gray.

Lapetus looked at Ethan oddly, answering as if he had spoken aloud. "His hair is not gray. It is black, the color of the wolf that I—"

"I am the same spirit but appear to you both differently," the young man answered.

Ethan's head continued to swim. Was this some sort of illusion? But he thought not. In his mind, he heard Aneira's voice whisper to him, *"Listen closely, Etienne, this is the way forward."*

"Why are we here?" he asked directly.

"Yes, how may we serve you?" Lapetus echoed with a bit more flourish.

"You both must listen and observe. As I attempted to tell you before, Lapetus, the path of the clan is shifting and evolving. You must evolve with it. Your Brother, here, will travel a new road, a unique one. But will, through blood, always be connected to the clan. As he learns, as he grows, as he evolves, you will all benefit. He was chosen with this purpose."

"I chose him," Lapetus almost lashed out with anger but then more sedately added, "I thought he would be a good addition to our Brotherhood."

The young man smiled at him almost lovingly, Ethan thought, though clearly as one might look at a child. "Lapetus, you are close to our spirit, but as in all things, you are guided unless you choose to break from us."

"No, no, of course," he muttered.

"You must allow this Brother to leave, to follow his path as we have foreseen. Do you understand me?"

Lapetus stared forward with no expression, though Ethan could feel much. As Lapetus had indicated, thoughts and emotions seemed more permeable in this enchanted place. He could feel a tumult of emotion, anger, resentment toward Geraint, and then beneath it, something more profound, fear. There was fear in him that what he knew, how he lived, would be taken from him. So, in response, with concentration, Ethan sent out a thought, one thought directly to him — *I offer you only peace, my Brother.*

Suddenly Lapetus turned toward him as though that thought had resulted in almost a physical impact. He saw a recognition in his eyes, then slowly he turned back, back to the youth sitting on the tree who claimed that he was the manifestation of the wolf spirit.

"Not claimed, am." He said distinctly and with a measure of disdain in his tone.

Lapetus stared forward, nodding. "I understand," he added softly, "and I accept."

And then the youth stood lightly atop the tree trunk, holding up his hands, palms flat, facing them, "Then manifest," he said with emphasis.

◆

In a swirl, Ethan found himself back atop that lonely hill surrounded by the men of the wolf clan. His hand was still securely grasping Lapetus' throat. Taking a deep breath, he looked into his Brother's eyes, not seeing fear but an odd expression of expectancy. Slowly, Ethan removed his hand, which now had transformed back into a merely human appendage again.

Lapetus stepped back, slowly rubbing his throat, but his eyes never left Ethan's face. "Kian, Balor, Taranis, we now return to our homeland."

Kian stepped in front of him, glowering at Ethan. "Return? Without—"

"Yes," Lapetus said with steel and resolve in his voice. "An agreement has been reached. They will go on, unencumbered by us. Do you understand me?"

Slowly, Ethan heard the men of the wolf clan, one by one, agree, albeit begrudgingly. And as Lapetus began to walk away, he first turned to Enid, eying her with a quick smile that disturbed Ethan more than he'd like to admit. "All my best, my Lady," he said quietly.

And then they were left, he and Enid, alone on that quiet hill, a soft breeze blowing Enid's cloak about her. Ethan turned to her, smiling. "Thank you, beloved. Without your skills, I don't believe we would have had this outcome."

She smiled at him softly and a bit sadly, he thought. "You met with him, didn't you, the wolf spirit?"

"Yes," he said slowly. "He brokered this deal."

"Brokered?" She laughed lightly, "You use such strange words. I had a sense of him near. I have seen him as well, though at another time. He spoke to me and told me I am tied to his spirit, as are you."

He lovingly put his hands on her arms, "It seems so, my love."

She nodded. "And now it is time for you to return to your life, your time, Ethan."

Ethan took a quick breath, knowing that at some point, this would happen. But the abruptness of it took him off guard. "It is difficult for me to leave you, Enid."

211

She smiled again, a few tears falling from her lovely amber eyes. "Yes, you always knew that we would have this ending. And I must have my husband back. We have much to discuss."

An unexpected sadness enveloped him, although he had achieved the best outcome for all involved. "I don't know how he will react."

She shrugged slightly, which he found deeply endearing. "I will soften his ire. And he too may have learned a bit from all this in his slumber."

"By osmosis?"

She smiled, "Another strange word." She reached up and kissed him softly on the lips. "Travel well, my sweet husband. May the future be kind to you."

Impulsively, Ethan swept Enid into his arms again, kissing her passionately as though it were the last time because he knew now that it was.

◆

And then he awoke. He breathed in sharply, steadying himself from the disorientation. Shakily, he stood from his sitting position. His heart was filled with so many emotions, so many he couldn't begin to sort through yet. But then he began to feel, to feel the discordant note in the air.

He steadied himself and then walked through the doorway and down the hall. It was quiet, but he knew they were in the den. As he entered the room, Erin's eyes flew to him in a panic, and then he saw the figure across the room in the dark suit standing in front of the window.

He turned around slowly, Lapetus' face breaking into a curious smile. "Well, Brother. I hope you don't mind me dropping by."

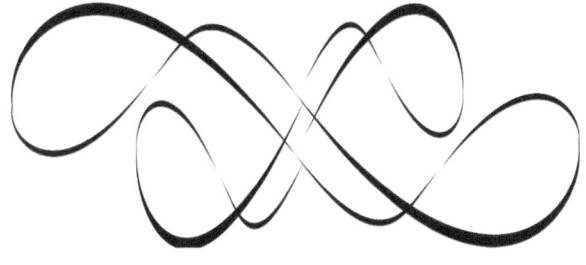

# Chapter 32

# THE SIGNS

T he ceiling fan spun languorously over the bed, and her head ached. In fact, more than that, it throbbed. She reached for her cell phone plugged in on the end table. It was Friday, already Friday. This afternoon, her flight would take her back to Arkansas. Where had the week gone?

♦

Ethan was drained and exhausted yet methodically sized up the situation in his den. He braced himself for a confrontation with this very old werewolf who stood so placidly in front of his patio window. Erin immediately rose to her feet, meeting him at the doorway where he stood. "He was here when I woke up." She whispered with such anxiety in her voice.

That, more than anything, made him want to splatter Lapetus' innards across the kitchen linoleum. How dare he invade his home.

But then, a fleeting remembrance of the peace they had just struck in the distant past, which now seemed like such a recent past, drifted almost intangibly across his mind. In consideration of this, perhaps he should give him a chance, one chance to explain himself.

His eyes locked onto his old nemesis. "What are you doing here?" He said with a quiet yet unmistakably menacing voice.

His tone, more than anything, he suspected, caused a slight smile to flicker across Lapetus' thin lips. "Me? Just passing through, Brother, and entertaining your Lady friend. Curious of you to leave her unattended for so long."

Ethan's eyes passed over Erin, and he felt a million things at once. He certainly hadn't planned for things to go this way. But then again, he hadn't planned. Whatever good he'd done for Enid, and he dearly hoped that was so, it had made things very complicated here.

He was not so evolved not to be affected by the fact that he'd spent the last several days in his wife's bed. Although she was a wife who had lived centuries ago, it was all too fresh for him.

"Erin," he said softly. "Do you mind waiting for me in the back?" He'd almost said bedroom, but even that felt somehow awkward now. Being with Enid again still affected him in so many ways that he had yet to sort out. Her eyes widened. "Please," he added. "This gentleman and I have some business to settle."

She looked at him oddly, so pale, so vulnerable, and that stung at him more than anything. This had not been his intention to come into her life and cause difficulties for her in any way.

"All right," she said softly, casting a quick glance back at Lapetus that Ethan had difficulty interpreting. And then she disappeared through the doorway that he had emerged from.

"Gentleman? That seems generous of you," he stated from across the room, where he'd continued to stare out the window.

214

"Why are you in my house?"

Then he spun around, smiling. "Less generous, Brother."

"I want you out," Ethan said flatly.

"No doubt," and then he returned his focus to the courtyard outside. "Lovely little picturesque place you have here. I wonder, do you ever read the signs?"

"Signs?"

"Yes, friend. Since I've been here, you've had two blue jays, several sparrows, and a crow. My mother was a great advocate of reading the signs of nature. You see, the blue jays denote change, the sparrow's abundance, and the crow. Well, that is the rub. You see, the crow denotes a choice between this world and another." And then his eyes narrowed as he stared directly at Ethan. "And you, my friend, have the smell of incantation about you as though you have been traveling through a realm of magic, not this world, surely."

Ethan sat down slowly in his rocking chair, the one he'd crafted himself years ago. His body ached basically everywhere. Evidently, the journey that he'd embarked on had taken much more out of him than he'd expected. "I'm not in the mood for riddles, Lapetus. Long ago, we made a pact, an agreement to stay out of each other's way. I'm wondering what in the world might have possessed you to break your word."

He shrugged, seeming entirely too light-hearted for the gravity of this exchange. "Am I in your way, Brother? As far as I can see, this is only a friendly visit, and if you want to know the truth, and I'd imagine you do by that scowl on your face, I didn't come to see you."

◆

She sat up in the bed, trying to clear her mind. It was foggy. In fact, everything seemed foggy. She'd attended several educational seminars at the beginning of the week, and then, something had happened.

Vaguely, she could remember becoming ill and ending up in a medical clinic near the convention center. Some kind of food poisoning, they'd said, giving her medicine. And she'd have to rest, rest until she went home.

Her head swam with dizziness as she walked across the room, opening the door that led out onto the balcony. She breathed the outside air in deeply, but her head still throbbed. Maybe if she ate something, she'd feel better on her flight back home.

◆

Again, Ethan's eyes fixed squarely on Lapetus. "What are you saying?" He didn't like this on the heels of what he'd just been through. It wasn't just poor timing. It was downright suspicious. He couldn't help but wonder if what they'd accomplished in the past had rippling effects in their present.

The tall, gaunt man just seemed to be eying everything with little reaction, a cold assessment. Yes, he certainly didn't want Kian around, but this one, and he hesitated to call him a man because it had been a very long time since either of them were men. Well, he was so much more dangerous.

"I'm talking about the woman."

"I realize that," he said sternly, not rising from his seated position.

"She seems — unrealized."

Ethan focused on him, "Curious word, Lapetus."

"I know who she is. I mean, who she was."

Inwardly, he drew a sharp breath. "Do you? Then you understand that if you come near her again, I will dismember you inch by inch and then incinerate you."

Again, Lapetus smiled lightly, "Vivid description, Brother. I mean her no harm. Just wondering really. You see, power, particularly relating to our kind, is monitored. Great power was sensed here and imagine my surprise when it was connected to my favorite couple. You and Lady Enid."

Slowly, he rose to his feet. "That is not Enid."

An odd, unreadable expression crossed his face. "You know, I always thought I'd be a better match for her than you were. You were so careful, cautious, never let her truly fly as she might have."

A coldness crept into his heart. If only, if only, he hadn't promised the elf-like being who purported to be the wolf spirit, given his vow. "I think we're done here, Lapetus."

He nodded slowly, "Well, yes, I see you're not in the mood to discuss this. And you seem tired, old friend," he said softly as he placed his fingertips on Ethan's shoulder. "I wonder where you've been that has depleted you so."

And then he turned, heading toward the front door. "Your Lady, give her my regards, will you, Geraint? And make sure you treat her well. After all, deep down, she'll always be one of us." And then he opened the door, shutting it firmly behind him.

Ethan sank back down into the rocker, feeling completely gutted. His mind could not firmly wrap around all that had occurred so quickly. He knew he should go to Erin to reassure her, but he didn't have it in him. It felt as though all he'd done was make a mess of everything, though he knew or at least hoped that was not the case.

He closed his eyes, trying to focus, and heard Brother Guidrade's voice from a distant place. "You've done well, Etienne. Be peaceful."

"Have I?" he sent the thought outward because he was not convinced, not at all.

◆

"Yeah, I'm feeling better, but this week was kind of a bust."

"That's okay, Erin. It was a life experience."

She smiled, sinking onto the bed. Just like her Mom to put a positive spin on everything. "I guess. It just wasn't what I hoped for, you know."

"Well, sometimes we have to adjust our trajectory when life hands us a curve."

She nodded, "Yeah, yeah, I think you're right. Love you, Mom."

"Love you too, baby. See you tonight."

"Okay," and then she hung up. She stared at the phone for a moment. It was troublesome, definitely felt like there was something she'd forgotten, forgotten something important.

◆

Erin didn't understand what was happening. The voices from the front of the house had stopped, and she heard a door shut or nearly slam, then quiet. She waited in Ethan's study, thinking that at any moment, he would come to her and explain things. But he didn't. There was just quiet, silence that stretched on. So, after what felt like an interminable amount of time, she decided to go up front.

When she entered the den, she saw immediately that the stranger had left, and, more oddly than that, Ethan was sitting all alone, motionless, in a chair.

"He's gone," he said quietly.

"I'm glad," she answered. "He disturbed me."

As she moved to stand in front of his chair, she noticed a peculiar smile had crossed his face. Almost sad, she thought. "Yes, well, he is a disturbing fellow."

"Who is he?" she asked, feeling so oddly disoriented.

And then he focused on her directly. "He's like me."

She hesitated, "Like you? Oh, you mean he's a were—"

He nodded, "Werewolf, lycanthrope, Brother of the blood," he said almost sarcastically.

"Not much of a Brother. You don't seem to like him much."

"Yes, well, not much to like there," he looked at her curiously. "Are you all right?"

"I don't know," she whispered. "I feel, I feel very strange, as though something has happened, but I don't remember anything."

He stood up, rather abruptly pulling her into his arms. "I'm sorry, Erin. I'm sorry. I believe I've been very selfish bringing you into my life, such as it is, the way I did. It wasn't fair to you."

"I don't know what you're saying," she said with genuine confusion.

"It's all right," he murmured, and then he began to kiss her intently as though nothing else mattered.

# Chapter 33

# A PUZZLE PIECE

He hadn't taken enough time to enjoy the moments was his thought as he held her so closely in his arms. He wondered what thoughts were passing through her mind. Did she regret him, regret the time they'd spent together?

"What are we going to do?" she asked softly.

He pulled her more securely against his body. He loved the feel of her lovely skin against his. "Do?" he asked.

"Yes," she said. "I'm supposed to be heading home Friday, but—"

"But," he echoed her words, waiting, wondering what indeed she would say.

"But things have changed. You and I, I mean. I couldn't possibly go back to the life I had before, not now."

"I see," he said softly, kissing the top of her head. He'd like to turn back the clock now, not have this conversation, but just return to holding her close. "Because of me?"

Then she sat up, her lovely ginger-colored hair falling around her bare shoulders. "You weren't just planning for this to be a quick affair, were you, Mr. Garraint?"

He smiled, lightly brushing her locks away from her cheek. "No, that's not what I planned, Miss Holt."

"So, what are we going to do?"

"We'll talk about it," he said, then he pulled her down to kiss her again and blot out whatever lay before them.

◆

An Uber would be picking her up in half an hour downstairs to bring her to the airport. She'd managed to eat half a po'boy for lunch, which helped stabilize her just a bit.

Erin thought about taking a quick walk outside and snapping a few more New Orleans pictures with her phone before she left, but she didn't feel like it. In fact, she didn't feel like doing much of anything. Such a strange, odd, disconnected emotion bordering on depression, something she was familiar with. After she gained her sight, there was a period when she just felt largely depressed, as though in the process of acclimating to the sighted world, something was lost, something important along the way that she couldn't account for.

That was how she was feeling now, like a puzzle piece that didn't quite fit anymore.

◆

She was still asleep when he got out of bed. His head throbbed with hunger, perhaps, with sadness, yes, that as well. They had five more days, five more days until she would be going home. Ethan sighed inwardly. The world, they claim in the Old Testament, was created in seven.

What could he do in five?

He wandered to the kitchen, but once he got there, he realized he'd lost his appetite. He sat at the small dinette table quietly in the darkness. Every day, they would go out and every day return here and spend the night together.

He would revel in her and memorize every glance, every nuance of her being, and then tuck it away in his soul. And on the last day, he would bring her back to her hotel and then kiss her softly.

Then he would cast his spell.

Ethan Garraint did not consider himself a practitioner of magic nor a spiritualist, but he had learned skills along the way. And while they were most instructive to him, the Cathars of Montségur did not teach him this particular brand of magic. It was his old friend, the Magician Houdin. While he was most often a Master of the sleight of hand, he was also a great warlock. And one stormy night, after two bottles of Cabernet, he began to teach him the art of mesmerism, specifically the technique of influencing memories.

He'd done it once before to Erin Holt, making her completely forget him when she regained her sight. But of course, those memories he'd restored again so recently.

But this time, he would completely erase his existence from her conscious mind and replace the past week's memories with something else. Ostensibly, he would let her go back to a simpler, kinder life where he was nothing to her. He would gift her this and, yes, perhaps tear his heart out in the process. But it wouldn't be the first time.

His mind turned back to his lovely Enid and the day she died, on her forty-first birthday. A virulent plague had swept the countryside to which he was immune, but he had held her all night, close to him, and heard her last breaths. Then he buried her and left his homeland behind.

It crossed his mind to join the clan of the wolves at that point, join with Lapetus, but something held him apart.

"We all have the path of the spirit to follow," Brother Guidrade had counseled him. "Even you, Etienne."

His beloved Brother had also told him that one day Enid would reincarnate on this earth, and that was true as well. But in five days, he was setting her free.

◆

There were whispers in her mind, disconnected whispers floating about that she did not understand.

*"Shouldn't we make plans of some sort?"*

*"We will, Erin, when the time is right."*

*"I just, I just want you to know what you mean to me. I love you, Ethan."*

And then a soft answer, *"And I love you."*

She paced the airport, waiting for the gate to open leading to her plane. Her head hurt, a headache she couldn't seem to rid herself of. It clung to her, and these odd, distracted thoughts nagged at her.

Maybe, maybe when she got back to Arkansas, things would right themselves again. But she hoped it rather than believed it. Just an odd, disconnected piece of a puzzle that didn't quite fit. Perhaps that was what she would always be.

But who did she want to be?

Such a question, one that she seldom really entertained. Who was she, and who would she be?

◆

"Why are we here?"

Ethan smiled at her, his eyes filled with some indiscernible emotion that she couldn't quite reach. "I wanted to talk to you here, Erin. Where things began."

She could feel something disturbing. It felt like a pain in her heart. "Ethan," she said haltingly.

"No," he spoke succinctly. "Sit down," he murmured. And she sunk onto the hotel bed. "Now listen to me, Erin. I want you to close your eyes."

"Why?" It felt like panic rising in her. Something was terribly wrong.

"Do you trust me?"

"Yes, yes, of course."

"Then please do as I ask." There was something in his voice, something so sad that made her hurt inside.

"All right," she whispered. And then she felt his hand on her forehead, right in the center, and the very next thing was darkness.

◆

Erin rested quietly in her window seat on the airplane. The two seats next to her were empty, but the plane did seem to be under booked. Her headache still persisted though it had ebbed into a dull ache, a bit of background noise. She felt sad, and she didn't know why. She felt lost, though she could connect it to nothing. She was not regretting nor looking forward to anything.

Life had lost its vibrancy and purpose. Maybe it was depression, and she would see someone when she got back about it, though her mind hesitated on the word home. Was it home in Arkansas?

What was and could be home for her?

She closed her eyes and then opened them again, just staring out the window at the clouds that the plane floated lightly above.

"Do you mind if I sit here?" She looked up and found herself staring into the face of a lovely blond woman with the most beautiful amber-colored eyes.

◆

"You know, Lady Enid has always been a remarkable person, Geraint. I believe you have always underestimated her. I wonder if you will make that mistake twice."

He'd forgotten it, something Lapetus had said to him before he left. It seems he hadn't even acknowledged it until now. He glanced around the house and thought he would sell it and leave soon. The city no longer entranced him as it once had. He looked at his watch. Erin's plane would be in the air now. She was heading home.

And he wondered with distraction how long that reality would feel like a knife in his gut, perhaps forever, perhaps.

◆

"Sure," she murmured as the lovely young woman settled in the seat next to her. She wore an off-white knit dress with her long golden hair hanging loose around her shoulders.

She smiled at Erin kindly. "You really don't remember."

"Remember? Do we know each other?" She asked with hesitation.

The lady shrugged, still smiling, almost as though she had a secret. "Sort of, Erin, Erin Holt. That is a pretty name."

"Thanks."

And then she reached out and unexpectedly grasped Erin's hand. "We're sisters in a way, but closer than most. You see, I didn't think he'd really do it."

"Do what?" Erin asked with complete confusion. But there was more. Her hand was hot where the young woman was touching her, and she could feel something inexplicable seeping into her skin.

"I guess he thought he was being noble in his way, but I think it's more important to be fair."

Erin looked at her with confusion. And on top of that, she was feeling so dizzy. "I don't understand."

"I traveled a long way to give you this." And then suddenly, the young woman opened her other hand. Erin could see from where she was that the most delicate blue flower was in her palm. "It's called a forget-me-not. It's for you, Erin, but understand if you inhale its fragrance, you will remember everything. And nothing will ever be the same again. But I came here because I think you deserve to choose." And then she slowly stood up, releasing her. "Open your hand, Erin," she said softly.

All Erin could do was stare into her mesmerizing brown eyes, so filled with light. And she did as she asked, opening her hand. The blond woman gently put the flower in it and then smiled. "I have to go now. My husband is waiting for me. Remember, it's your choice."

And then she turned and walked away. It took a moment for Erin to get hold of herself, but when she turned to look down the aisle where the woman had gone, she saw that she had vanished. She took a quick breath and then stared down at the flower. *"A puzzle piece that doesn't quite fit,"* a soft voice whispered in her mind.

Erin didn't take very much time. She simply lifted the flower to her face and inhaled deeply.

*Finis*

## The Lady in the Blue Dress
6 x 9 Softcover & Hardcover 214 pages
ISBN 978-1-61342-600-5
ISBN (Hardcover) 978-1-61342-418-6

When she was a child, Mika Devalieur was introduced to her grandmother's most precious possession — a priceless and mysterious painting that she simply called The Lady in the Blue Dress. Upon Adele St. Clair's death, the painting is left in the care of her granddaughter with only one stipulation. Mika must hand over the family heirloom to a total stranger. Mika Devalieur desperately wants to deny her beloved grandmother's last request, but she can't. Torn between her Gran's last wishes and her desire to hold onto the Lady, she ultimately journeys to rural Virginia, where an enigmatic man shows her that this painting is only the beginning.

What quickly becomes clear is that James Clairmont knows much more about her and the Lady than he is letting on. He begins to slowly unravel a powerful supernatural connection that spans three generations of her family. Mika finds herself desperate to uncover the entire truth before she falls in love with a man filled with so many secrets — secrets about him, about her, and most especially about The Lady in the Blue Dress.

## Dumaine Street
6 x 9 Softcover & Hardcover 306 pages
ISBN 978-1-61342-902-0
ISBN (Hardcover) 978-1-61342-416-2

Voices in her head, catastrophic emotions, hallucinations — Rebecca Wells is more than convinced that she is losing her mind. And as a last-ditch effort, she contacts a self-professed counselor who seems convinced he can help.

Gabriel Sutton has abandoned the world of medicine to navigate a realm filled with psychic phenomena. Diagnosing Becca with extreme empathic abilities, he struggles to help her stabilize her gifts while trying desperately not to fall in love with his patient.

From the realm of vulnerability into a crusade to use their profound gifts to rescue others from peril on the other side of death, these two follow an astonishing and unpredictable path into each other's hearts.

## The Tethering
*A Portent of Crows*
6 x 9 Softcover & Hardcover 201 pages
ISBN 978-1-61342-599-2
ISBN (Hardcover) 978-1-61342-419-3

Deborah Brandt's beloved Aunt Gena always told her that she was special, a bit different, and would have to live her life, unlike other people. Of course, this she disregarded as the ramblings of her lovely but notably eccentric aunt. Although there were the things that Aunt Gena said that seemed true — like Deborah being sensitive to energy shifts, having potentially psychic impressions, and dreaming of a spirit guide — none of it could be real. But the most ridiculous thing that her Aunt Gena told her before she died was that someone special was out there for her. She said that he was an extraordinary man who was not only her perfect match but someone who she would learn from so that they could help the world in difficult times. How ridiculous! It sounds like a fairy tale, and no such person exists.

Daniel Wren is unique. He has been raised and trained from a young age to hone his psychic gifts. He lives in a world unimagined by most. And he has been waiting for years to contact his counterpart, soulmate, if you will. But the problem is that she is painfully unaware of the type of life that he lives and the life she would be entering into if they came together.

His dilemma becomes how best to proceed. How can he win her over and move forward before outside forces take that decision away from him?

### Travels into the Breach
*Accounts of a Reluctant Mystic*
6 x 9 Softcover & Hardcover 171 pages
ISBN 978-1-61342-323-3
ISBN (Hardcover) 978-1-61342-417-9

At first glance, his life seems quiet, serene, and even uneventful. Malachi McKellan, a 65-year-old widower and author of esoteric books, lives largely as a recluse in a house situated just off the banks of Bayou St. John in New Orleans. But unbeknownst to most, he is also a bit of a detective, a specific kind of detective whose specialty is psychic attacks. Alongside his lifelong companion and spirit guide Simon Tull, a 19th-century, 20-something English gent, Malachi battles the unseen, and is an unacknowledged hero to the most vulnerable. Most of the population have no idea what is really happening beneath the surface of the world in which they live.

In this collection of adventures, Malachi McKellan and Simon Tull wage war against the most insidious elements of the paranormal. In *The Three*, Malachi and Simon come to the aid of a young woman being victimized by a group of dark witches. An old apartment building is the scene of an unimaginable battle against monstrous forces in *The Lost Soul*. Malachi and Simon find themselves strategizing against a psychic vampire in *Obsession*, and *The Hotel* turns back time to the 1980s where Malachi confronts a demonic spirit. In *Between*, a past life is revisited as Malachi attempts to rescue a beloved sister from committing her existence to vengeance, and *The Wedding* takes a personal turn when Malachi must confront painful truths while endeavoring to protect his niece from a potentially devastating union.

Travel into the breach with a pair of paranormal warriors who choose to confront overwhelming forces on a battlefield unsuspected by most.

### Gravier's Bookshop
*A New Orleans Paranormal Mystery (#1)*
6 x 9 Softcover & Hardcover 172 pages
ISBN 978-1-61342-288-5
ISBN (Hardcover) 978-1-61342-411-7

Max Gravier had no intention of becoming a recluse, but after his wife's death it seems his life is heading in that direction. He spends his time running Gravier's Bookshop on Magazine Street and occasionally on the quiet helps the police solve a crime with his psychic sensitivities. That is until he answers Caroline Breslin's call, a cry for help out of his dreams that draws him into a fierce battle for a young woman's soul.

In this first installment of The New Orleans Paranormal Mystery series, Caroline Breslin, an amazingly gifted empath, is determined to strike out on her own and has moved out from the protection of her family home. All is going extremely well until, of course, she comes under siege from a devastating supernatural attack. The last thing Caroline wants is to run back to her family for help, even though she is painfully in over her head. What she really needs is a knight in shining armor — or maybe just that guy that keeps haunting her dreams.

Join them and the whole Breslin family psychic clan in this first installment of The New Orleans Paranormal Mystery Series where you'll travel into a new world just a few steps into the turbulent realm of the unseen.

### The Hotel Mandolin
*A New Orleans Paranormal Mystery (#2)*
6 x 9 Softcover & Hardcover 146 pages
ISBN 978-1-61342-290-8
ISBN (Hardcover) 978-1-61342-412-4

Peril is wrapped up in the most enticing of disguises in *The Hotel Mandolin*, the second installment of The New Orleans Paranormal Mystery series. It's opulent, classic, and one of the most renowned hotels nestled deep in New Orleans' famous business district, but something is amiss at The Hotel Mandolin.

PI Peter Norfleet is calling out the big guns to help him investigate a recent suicide at the famous establishment — his good friend Max Gravier, a formidable psychic, and his girlfriend, Caroline Breslin, a talented empath. But none of them can seem to scratch the surface of this puzzle, no one except Cassie Breslin, Caroline's clairvoyant mother, who has somehow tapped into an unexpected connection with a tragic ghost from the turn of the century. And the more she uncovers, the more dangerous and malevolent the mystery becomes

## The House at Pritchard Place
*A New Orleans Paranormal Mystery (#3)*
6 x 9 Softcover & Hardcover 138 pages
ISBN 978-1-61342-292-2
ISBN (Hardcover) 978-1-61342-413-1

Nothing is really wrong with the old Warrick House on Dante St. except that there most certainly is. Nothing is exactly wrong with its new mysterious owner except that Elise is sure that something doesn't add up. It isn't obvious, but sometimes the most dangerous things aren't.

In the third installment of The New Orleans Paranormal Mystery series, with the help of her very psychic sister and her children, the Breslin clan, Elise Ashford is about to embark on a wild rescue mission straight into another dimension that will land her squarely somewhere she doesn't expect, right back into her past. She'll land full circle; in a childhood home whose memory still haunts her to this day -- *The House at Pritchard Place.*

## Treading on Borrowed Time
6 x 9 Softcover & Hardcover 223 pages
ISBN 978-1-61342-214-4
ISBN (Hardcover) 978-1-61342-436-0

For Julia Moreau, life seems complicated. Emerging from a failed marriage and managing a lifetime of diabetes, she lives alone in her childhood home where she communicates with the spirit of her Great Aunt Lilia. But Julia doesn't have a clue what complicated is until she is thrust into being the key chess piece in a match between two powerful men of extraordinary abilities on the wild hunt for a mystical creature hidden in the heart of New Orleans' French Quarter. Will Julia lose her soul to the karma of a devastating past life or her heart to the love of a man driven by dark forces? What is clear is that whichever way she turns she is *Treading on Borrowed Time*.

## Sanctuary of Echoes
6 x 9 Softcover & Hardcover 371 pages
ISBN 978-1-61342-211-3
ISBN (Hardcover) 978-1-61342-409-4

Ghosts unacknowledged do not sleep.

Corey Knight has resigned herself to a quiet, reclusive life spent living out the rest of her days in her childhood home on the fringes of New Orleans' French Quarter. But the unexpected specter of her deceased father plunges her into a mad quest for a missing supernatural weapon unearthed long ago. And unfortunately, her only ally is a lost love she once betrayed.

Iain Shaw returns to New Orleans, a city he abandoned a decade before while fleeing a devastating past. Here, he is forced to confront it again in the visage of the woman he once adored - one that he is now determined to get back at any cost.

Follow them both in a wild paranormal tale of discovery and redemption as they confront and unearth the echoes of a buried and unyielding truth that once tore them irreparably apart.

**A Quiet Moment**
6 x 9 Softcover & Hardcover 273 pages
ISBN 978-1-61342-326-4
ISBN (Hardcover) 978-1-61342-435-3

Jacob Wyss is caught in a rut, in fact on the verge of being engulfed by it. After an excruciating and disillusioning divorce, his life as an artist in a sleepy-college town at the foot of the Appalachian Mountains has become quiet, routine, and maddening in its predictability. One wintry day, his deep restlessness drives him out in precarious conditions to a largely empty bookstore nearly devoid of another living soul, nearly.

Aimee Marston isn't like everyone else. On the surface, she lives a sedate life working as a feature writer for a small local newspaper in addition to several other editorial jobs to help make ends meet. But just beneath, her existence is largely not her own. She is a sensitive, an empathetic psychic, guided by her calling to use her gifts to help others. Unfortunately, as a result, her secretiveness has made her defensive, protective of herself, and prevented her from having much of a life.

A psychic call for help sends Aimee out on a freezing January morning where her destiny and Jacob's collide sending both their lives spiraling onto an unexpected and often disturbing track. Two lonely souls connect, not by accident, but by design. Theirs is the intersection of two spiritual paths, two lovers who must struggle to overcome the phantoms of a past life, as well as the challenges of their own inner demons to carve out an extraordinary future together.

## A Ghost of a Chance

6 x 9 Softcover & Hardcover 230 pages
ISBN 978-1-61342-162-8
ISBN (Hardcover) 978-1-61342-440-7

You never know what's coming next.

Jack Brennan, an ambitious high-powered attorney, dies. But that's not the end, rather only the beginning. He finds himself constrained to an inexplicable afterlife as an earth-bound spirit trapped in an old Virginia farmhouse. His only companion is a very much living, reclusive writer of campy vampire novels. The maddening problem is that Hallie does not know he is there, nor that he is somewhat reluctantly falling in love with her.

Hallie Barkly is recovering from a painful and disillusioning divorce. Out of the ashes of her former life, she has managed to somehow forge a career and exorcise her demons by writing under the pseudonym of Sebastian Winters. Slowly, she is awakening to the fact that she is not alone.

Their lives intersect, and two unconventional lovers are brought together under insurmountable circumstances. Together they must battle an unseen force hell-bent on possessing Hallie's life and bridge death itself to make possible what cannot be — to find a chance.

## Dragonflies - Journeys into the Paranormal
6 x 9 Softcover & Hardcover 176 pages
ISBN 978-1-88756-072-6
ISBN (Hardcover) 979-8-32548-418-6

In every form of creation, there is a blueprint for living, for experience, for interpretation. In flight, they can twist, turn, alter direction, pause in midair, and even fly backward. The dragonfly is the master of adaptability. They are a living prism, refracting light, and color, seemingly shifting their essence.

The lesson the dragonfly gives is that life is never what it appears to be.

In "The Wizard," as a novice practitioner of magic, Aurora Finn finds herself battling against the illusions of a powerful wizard intent on separating her from the world she knows. "The Sojourners" is a gentle story of a mother and daughter whose tenancy in an old Virginia farmhouse uncovers the trials and sorrows of its former occupants. A bookstore clerk gets an extraordinary customer on Halloween night in "Late One Night at Berstrums Books." In "The Tear," a woman coping with her fatal illness unknowingly begins a track on a mystical journey that will entirely restructure her vision of the world.

These stories follow the path of the dragonfly imbued with the momentum and energy of change, taking a winding and treacherous journey that ultimately leads to truth buried beneath perception.

## Breaking Through the Pale
6 x 9 Softcover 134 pages
ISBN 978-1-88756-045-0

Journey with metaphysical author Evelyn Klebert into a collection of short stories that travel beyond the pale into the unpredictable realm of the paranormal.

In "A Grey Mourning," a disillusioned man encounters a mysterious being on the foggy streets of New Orleans. "Contact" is a tale of automatic writing, when a young artist establishes communication with a spirit guide, and the victim of a car crash unravels the true nature of her existence in "Dancing on the Threshold." The final tale is called "Isolation," in which a confused and disoriented woman finds herself in an old, quaint house where she must piece together the mystical implications surrounding her predicament.

## Explanations
6 x 9 Softcover 82 pages
ISBN 978-1-93493-515-6

In this, her second poetry collection, Evelyn Klebert takes us down the intricate path of a personal journey. Life with its particular struggles, pitfalls, and ultimately triumphs clearly begins to mirror a universal path, the quest for answers that we all ultimately pursue. In this reflective, esoteric collection we can all explore and seek some of life's elemental mysteries and hopefully when all is said and done emerge with some *Explanations*.

## The Witches' Own
6 x 9 Softcover & Hardcover 140 pages
ISBN 978-1-61342-058-4
ISBN (Hardcover) 978-1-61342-428-5

On the surface things seem quiet and serene in the picturesque coastal village of Kilmarnock, Virginia. But something unseen roams its lush forests as the past and present collide and the unthinkable begins to wreak its vengeance. Young Lucy Bonner is executed for witchcraft in the town's distant and brutal past. Her death triggers an unholy chain of events which grasp at the restless heart of novelist Peter McQuade, spurring him towards a quest to uncover the dark and terrifying truth.

## The Left Palm
*And Other Halloween Tales of the Supernatural*
6 x 9 Softcover & Hardcover 122 pages
ISBN 978-1-93493-556-9
ISBN (Hardcover) 978-1-61342-442-1

Halloween is the time of year when that veil between worlds is thinned, and you can just catch a quick glimpse into the realm of the unknowable. In this collection of short stories, Evelyn Klebert takes you to a place where ordinary life splinters into the sphere of the paranormal.

The journey begins with one woman's unstoppable quest for vengeance against a supernatural creature in "Wolves" and continues in an old historical graveyard where a horrifying discovery is uncovered in "Emma Fallon." In "The Soul Shredder," a psychiatrist's unusual patient opens his eyes to a disturbing new view of reality, while in "Wildflowers," a woman strikes up a supernatural friendship with impossible implications. And in "The Left Palm," a fortuneteller in the French Quarter receives a most unexpected and terrifying customer.

## White Harbor Road
*And Other Tales of Paranormal Romance*
6 x 9 Softcover & Hardcover 152 pages
ISBN 978-1-61342-066-9
ISBN (Hardcover) 978-1-61342-441-4

A psychic soul mate, a time traveler, a horror writer, and an enigmatic stranger take a selection of resilient, life-battered heroines to a place of paranormal healing and transformation. In this collection of short stories, *White Harbor Road* is the last stop where life's burdens and hardships evolve into something unexpected.

## Considerations
6 x 9 Softcover 84 pages
ISBN 978-1-88756-062-7

Sometimes the struggle to understand the meaning and complexities of living comes down to a single moment of introspection or a fleeting yet meaningful reflection. This collection of poetry by Evelyn Klebert takes you down a winding path of self-discovery where the resolution may not always be absolute, but the journey is indeed unforgettable. It a wide and varied map of inspired poetry for your examination and consideration.

More Books by Evelyn Klebert

**Appointment with the Unknown**
*The Hotel Stories*
6 x 9 Softcover & Hardcover 155 pages
ISBN 978-1-61342-360-8
ISBN (Hardcover) 978-1-61342-421-6

A hotel, for most, represents a normal place, a predictable realm of commonality. One might even go as far to say a safe space, the reliable where nothing particularly unusual is expected to happen. Or is it? Dimensional traveling, spirit guides, mystical storms, and soul mates separated by time are only a few elements dotting this supernatural landscape. Drop into a collection of romantic paranormal stories where that place of commonality is only the threshold, the jumping-off point, for extraordinary adventures into the unknown.

Visit Evelyn's website at:
www.evelynklebert.com

Cornerstone Book Publishers
www.cornerstonepublishers.com